DEAD MAN IN HEAD

A Village Mystery

J.E. Rohrer

Ordering Information
The Books in the Dead Man series by J.E.
Rohrer are available from lulu.com

This book is dedicated to all the people in the
world who are afflicted with serious and
persistent mental illness.

CHAPTER 1. WHEN IS A TURKEY NOT A TURKEY?

The poor fellow was trying to push a freezer across Main Street. You might think I am making this up, but it is the absolute truth. The freezer was resting on some sort of dolly that had four small wheels. The man pushing it looked a bit wild, with his long, greasy hair and ragged clothes. No criticism is intended in describing him as greasy and ragged. If you were pushing a refrigerator up the middle of the street, you would be ragged and greasy in a short period of time. After all, it was sweaty work and hard on your clothes.

When I saw him, I was about to climb into my car after picking up a few groceries at the Sentry store. The freezer man had managed to back up a line of traffic, which was understandable, since people pushing freezers on dollies were bound to move at a slower rate of speed than the more common vehicles were able to achieve. He was scowling as he strained to push the freezer slowly forward. Or, perhaps, he was scowling because he knew the drivers of the cars behind him were staring and probably cursing him quietly.

The light changed and it was his turn to move across Main Street. The freezer moved forward at a snail's pace. I could easily imagine the impatience felt by the drivers in those cars; don't you just hate it when you know you won't make it through a perfectly good green light because someone in front of you is moving too slowly? On the other hand, the man pushing the freezer was doing the best he could, under the circumstances.

At any other time in my life, I would have just stood there and watched. This was not because I am lazy (though I am) or because I am insensitive (guilty again), but because I am not a fast thinker in crisis situations. On this particular day, my synapses were firing a little more quickly than usual, so I threw my groceries in the car then ran out in the street to give the man some help.

He glared at me when I started pushing, but said nothing. No doubt, he was saving his breath. He did move his pushing position

WHEN IS A TURKEY NOT A TURKEY?

slightly to the left, which gave me room to get a better angle on the right side. Together, we managed to pick up the pace a little, though not very much. I am an over-fifty, semi-retired college professor who has never lifted weights in his life, so the strength I brought to the task was far less than a working man might have expected. The man pushing the freezer had the look of a working man; his clothes were dungarees and a plaid shirt and he wore heavy boots. Though it was November in Wisconsin, he had on no jacket. He had worked up a good sweat performing his task, so a jacket would have been too warm. I, on the other hand, wore a black blazer, blue shirt with a button-down collar, and chinos. Fortunately, I was also wearing my usual foot-gear: Red Wing walking shoes. These shoes had good tread on them and were ideal for pushing freezers.

The air was brisk; it might have been about 40 degrees outside. The frost had melted off the road already, since it was about nine in the morning. Our first snow had not yet fallen, though with Thanksgiving only two days away, the possibility of a blizzard could not be ruled out. All in all, it was good weather for pushing a freezer up the road.

"Hey, this thing's heavy," I said, just making conversation. My co-worker ignored me. Who could blame him? That kind of comment, where one stated the obvious, was a form of low-key humor commonly heard in the Midwest. However, when you were engaged in an arduous task, dumb jokes were not funny.

"What you got in here, turkeys?" I tried again to make conversation.

"Just….one..," he replied.

"Must be a big one!"

"Yup…big…..turkey. For sure."

By this time we were in the middle of the intersection. Perhaps what happened next was due to the distraction I caused by making conversation with the freezer man. On the other hand, the fact that I was not physically very strong might be the only explanation necessary. Whatever the reason, my side of the freezer was not keeping up with the side being pushed by the wild looking man. The bulky burden began to turn to the right. The street sloped downward there, which made the freezer difficult to control. Suddenly, it was

WHEN IS A TURKEY NOT A TURKEY?

rolling downhill.

Not wanting it to go rolling down Main Street on its own, I quickly shifted around to the front end of the freezer and dug in my heels. My shoes slid on the damp road as the freezer ignored my efforts and picked up speed. I lowered my center of gravity and pushed down harder on my feet and, at the same time, tried to push harder against the freezer. Unfortunately, the freezer just kept going.

Glancing over my shoulder, I saw a pickup truck close behind me. To avoid being pinned against it by the freezer, I scrambled on top, holding on to the strap that held it to its wheels. As soon as I leaped aboard, the freezer banged into the pickup. Its weight would not let it stop there, however. The other end of the freezer now swung around and we, the freezer and I, continued down Main Street.

My primary concern was to avoid allowing my hands or feet to be crushed as we banged off cars on either side of the street, picking up speed and caroming down the hill like a steel bearing in a pinball machine. The hill had just enough slope and the street was just slippery enough to allow the freezer-on-wheels to pick up a good rate of speed. We shattered glass, dented fenders, and tore off side mirrors on both sides of the street as our acceleration increased. I use the term 'we' because by this time my freezer and I had become quite close. We had bonded, so to speak. Jumping off would have been dangerous, so I hung on for dear life. The freezer was protecting me from the hard surface of the street, even as its increasing speed threatened me with consequences even more dire.

We broadsided a blue sedan in front of the city building, giving it a deep dent in the driver's side door. Just at that moment, a couple of police detectives I knew were walking out of the city building. Sergeant Schmidt was holding a cardboard cup of coffee, which she dropped when she saw what was happening. Whether it was the sight of someone she knew riding a freezer down Main Street or whether it was the damage done to her car that upset her the most, I couldn't say. But the scream she let loose may have provided a clue about what was upsetting her: "Schumacher!" That's my name. Since she did not shout "Mr. Schumacher" or "Professor Schumacher," I had to assume that she was upset with me again. The woman was biased against me for reasons I have never understood.

The freezer pinwheeled, so I lost sight of Schmidt and her partner, Sergeant Broder. We smashed some headlights and dented a few more fenders before reaching the bridge. For those of you who are not familiar with our little town, Fort Atkinson, let me describe the setting at this point in the story. Fort Atkinson has a nice little river running through the downtown area. The city's leadership has invested in creating a 'Riverwalk' that is quite attractive. The bridge connects one side of the downtown area with the other side. From the center of the bridge, you can look down to the see the Riverwalk and a few shops. It is really very picturesque.

The key point here is that the bridge rose a bit as it crossed the river. The hill down which I had been traveling reached its low point at the foot of the bridge. Despite the momentum we had achieved, we were not going over the bridge. Where, then, were we going?

DEAD MAN IN HEAD

The answer, as it turned out, was to the left side of the bridge. The freezer was moving quickly when it reached the foot of the bridge. It did not hesitate when the street began to rise, but shot to the left and off the road, taking out a chunk of cement railing and aiming for a concrete loading dock ten feet below.

I held on tightly while we were airborne. Some people say that your life passes before your eyes in the brief moment before imminent death, but those people probably were faster thinkers than I was. My mind just went blank until we struck the loading dock with a crash. The wheels of the dolly flew in all directions as we bounced and skidded off the edge of the loading dock into the river, then sank like a stone.

Fortunately, the river was not more than fifteen feet deep at that location. I say this was 'fortunate,' because I forgot to let loose of the strap until after the freezer came to a stop on the bottom of the river. Belatedly realizing my mistake, I gave a frenzied push with my legs and shot upward through the wet darkness.

Splashing around on the surface, with

WHEN IS A TURKEY NOT A TURKEY?

water obscuring my glasses, I was at first unsure which direction led toward the loading dock. Shouts got my attention and I began to stroke awkwardly toward the sound. My clothes were sodden and the water was very cold, so I tired quickly. Fortunately, the loading dock was nearby and, with the last of my remaining energy, I managed to reach out and grasp a helping hand that pulled me out of the water.

The hand belonged to Sergeant Broder. He led me back to the city building and took me inside. A blanket materialized from somewhere and I gratefully wrapped it around myself. Even so, I was shivering and felt light-headed.

Eventually, EMTs came and checked me over. Finding no cuts, abrasions, broken bones, or other injuries, they prescribed hot coffee and departed. My cell phone had disappeared, so I asked Broder if he would call my wife Betty and tell her where I was. I didn't really want to try to explain the situation to her; let Broder do that if he could.

After Broder made the call, he and Schmidt led me into one of their interrogation rooms. Broder was polite, as he always was.

DEAD MAN IN HEAD

For the first time, it occurred to me that this might not mean he was a nice guy; maybe his job was to be the 'good cop' and Schmidt's job was to be the 'bad cop.' If so, Schmidt was type-cast because there was no doubt in my mind that she was downright nasty.

After we were seated at the table in the interrogation room with me wrapped in a blanket and drinking coffee, Broder began by asking me to explain what happened.

"Well, this guy was pushing a freezer across Main Street up by the Sentry store, so I gave him a hand."

"That was your idea of being helpful?" Schmidt asked with a sneer. "Wrecking a bunch of cars and throwing his freezer into the river?"

Broder interrupted. "Tell me about the man you helped. Who was he?"

"Never saw him before."

"What did he look like?"

"Wait a minute. You mean he's gone?"

"Mr. Schumacher," Broder said gently, "all the witnesses said you were alone on the freezer when it was rolling down Main Street."

"Of course I was! The other guy never got

on the freezer!" Sometimes, these cops acted like I was nuts and it was very irritating. "I just got up there to avoid being crushed. I lost sight of him when we lost control of the darn thing."

"Can you describe this other man to us?"

"He was kind of grubby. Had on work clothes. Didn't look any too clean, frankly. I just figured he was pushing the freezer because he couldn't afford to have the thing moved on a truck."

"That brings me to my next question, Mr. Schumacher. Why was this man pushing a freezer through the center of town in the middle of the street?"

"He said he had his Thanksgiving turkey in there."

"Wouldn't it have been easier just to carry the turkey?"

"He said it was a really big turkey."

Schmidt slammed her fist down on the table. "This is the craziest story I ever heard," she growled. "And there aren't two people in this town crazy enough to push a freezer down the middle of the street. Admit it, Schumacher:

there is no other guy. You pulled this stunt on your own."

"I never saw the guy before today or his freezer!" Was this my reward for trying to do a good deed? "I was just giving a guy a push. You know, like we do when somebody is stuck in a snowdrift."

Broder leaned back in his chair. "Yes, Mr. Schumacher, I see what you mean. However, when we push someone out of a snowdrift we try not to damage seven cars and end up in the river."

He had a point. Somehow, my good deed had gone wrong, though I was having trouble figuring out exactly where I had made my mistake.

At this point the door to the interrogation room opened and a uniformed officer beckoned to Schmidt. She stepped out for a couple of minutes, then returned with a grin on her face. This was not looking good.

"Mister Schumacher," she announced. "You will be happy to know that the guys from the service station managed to winch that freezer of yours out of the river. It's on the loading dock now."

WHEN IS A TURKEY NOT A TURKEY?

"That's nice, but I would have left it down there until spring. That water is too cold to be working in if you don't have to."

"I just bet you would have preferred to leave it down there," Schmidt said, "considering what's inside it. Would you mind telling us again what you put in there?"

"I didn't put anything in there. The guy I was helping had a big turkey in there."

"The guy nobody saw put a turkey in there? More likely you put something in there. Only it wasn't a Thanksgiving turkey. It was a corpse, frozen solid."

Needless to say, it was a long time before they let me go home.

CHAPTER 2. THE ASSIGNMENT

The phone rang while I was cussing at the cat. Our main cat was an orange tabby named Fritter who had been living with us for about a year after we rescued her from a rain-swept parking lot in Iowa. Fritter was a very nice cat. However, Betty and I had been concerned that Fritter might get lonely when we weren't around the house, so we decided to acquire a kitten. Besides, we didn't play with Fritter enough and we assumed that having a little buddy would let us off the hook. Another important concern was Betty's need for her own cat. Fritter had always been my cat, by Fritter's choice, and Betty felt left out. Betty wanted a cat that would sit in her lap and allow petting and hugging. Fritter rarely allowed Betty to do that.

As a consequence of these pressing concerns, we picked up another orange tabby cat, whom we named Bucky. For those of you

THE ASSIGNMENT

who don't know the important facts of life, the mascot for the football team at of the University of Wisconsin is called Bucky. Since we were living in Wisconsin and since Betty had once attended UW, we named the new cat Bucky.

Bucky was lovable, but he was also a pain in the neck. He got into more trouble than Fritter had at the same age. Bucky would jump on my legs and dig in his claws. He scratched the furniture much more than Fritter ever had. He would throw things onto the floor. He would try to run out the door when he was supposed to stay inside. And worst of all, he would get up in the middle of the night and make noise when we were trying to sleep. Betty loved Bucky. So did I, but sometimes I cussed at him.

The phone rang while I was giving Bucky a lecture about not clawing my suit. I rarely bought a new suit, but at the rate Bucky was damaging this one I might be forced to replace it sooner than I wanted.

"Hello?" I asked the phone with some irritation at being interrupted in the middle of a lecture. "Professor Schumacher, please" a

15

voice said.

"Speaking."

"This is Jim Jones, vice president at the Medical University of Madison. We met briefly when you were investigating a research problem we were having."

"I remember." That little situation had been a sticky wicket, as the British say. And Jones had not helped one bit. He was a bureaucrat who had developed highly refined skills in covering his pitootie. That may not sound impressive, but given the enormity of his pitootie, you can be sure that his skills in that regard had to be Olympic-class.

Jones cleared his throat noisily, then said, "We, eh, were wondering if we might be able to, er, ask your assistance on a little problem we are facing here in Madison."

My silence was motivated less by reluctance than by shock. The Medical University of Madison, MUM for short, and I had not parted on the best of terms. Yet, here they were asking for my help. This was very odd.

Jones broke the silence. "Of course, we want to assure you that we at MUM, hmm, have the utmost regard, er, for your abilities. That little difference of opinion we had, hmm, was not of your doing. Of course, you understand."

I almost felt sorry for the weasel. He clearly was squirming.

"What can I do for you, Jim?"

Jones clearly was relieved that the ice was broken. "Well, as you know, we do a lot of research here and always take great pains to comply with all federal requirements. In fact, we are eager to go the extra mile to meet the spirit of federal regulations regarding patient rights and safety."

Yeah, right, I thought, especially after that blowup when you got caught being a little too cozy with the pharmaceutical industry. My finest hour was when I turned up the dirt on that crowd.

"Jim, you can skip the PR," I said. "What's up?"

"Hmm. Well, you may remember an incident a few weeks ago in which a man was found dead inside a freezer. It happened right there where you live, in Fort Atkinson."

DEAD MAN IN HEAD

"I remember." Darn right. The cops were far too rough on me. It would be a long time before I forgave them. "So? What about it?"

"Hmm. That dead man was enrolled in one of our research projects."

"Was he, now? That's interesting. And all deaths have to be reported, just in case they are caused by the research."

"That is correct."

"And the feds are being especially watchful over you guys, given the recent scandal."

"I wish you wouldn't use that word. It was hardly a scandal."

"Did the feds tell you that you had to find an independent investigator to look into this suspicious death?"

"You are very perceptive, Professor Schumacher."

"Why me?"

"Hmm. Well, the federal oversight agency regards you as being beyond any possible influence from the University, given that we were on opposing sides the last time we spoke."

THE ASSIGNMENT

"They are right about that; I am as independent as they come."

"Also, they knew from the newspaper accounts that you lived in Fort Atkinson, so hiring you would save on travel expenses."

That reason for choosing me was a little less flattering. Maybe I could get even for the insult by charging them a large fee.

"My usual fee is a thousand a day," I announced as if I had a 'usual fee.'

"That will be acceptable," Jones replied without hesitation. Perhaps I should have charged him more. "We will fax a contract to you immediately."

"Can you give me some more background on the situation? Of course, I will need to study the description of the research project, get the name and bio of the investigator, and have all of the information that was provided to the feds."

"We will run that information over to you by courier today. In brief, the situation is this: the research involved psychiatric patients…"

"Psych patients!" Vulnerable populations are supposed to be given special protection.

"The experiment involved a combination

of medications and psychotherapy given to subjects sharing a similar delusion. The medications themselves were not experimental," he hastened to add. "The novel dimension to the research was that the subjects were all chosen because they believed in the same kind of paranoid delusion. They all believed that they could see deceased persons."

"They saw dead people?"

"That's right."

"Well, that's interesting, but not outrageous. Tell me, Jim, what is the real problem here? Psychotic patients live dangerous lives and accidents happen. Sometimes, unfortunately, they end up dead. The feds know that. So, why have they taken the unprecedented step of demanding an independent investigation?"

Jones hesitated, then laid it on the line. "Prior to the discovery of the deceased, one of the subjects complained that he was not fully informed about the purposes of the research before he agreed to participate. He said all of the subjects were misled, or they would not have participated. He made this complaint to the federal authorities. Then, a short time later, one of the other subjects was found dead. The oversight agency is concerned that serious irregularities might have been occurring in this project."

"It sounds to me like they have reason to wonder about that." I sighed. "Okay, Jim, I will need access to information that normally is kept confidential. I need to know the names of the subjects, so that I can interview them and find out what really happened."

Jones was silent for a moment. "We had hoped you would not pursue the investigation in this way, but even so we anticipated your request. We are forced to comply. The names and latest contact information for the experimental subjects will be in the packet we are sending you. We are also faxing you a confidentiality agreement that you must sign and return to us. It will be part of the contract between the University and yourself."

"Fair enough. If I have any more questions after studying the material, I'll give you a call."

"Please do. Despite our past differences, I hope you understand that we truly want to protect the interests of any persons who participate in our research projects." It sounded like a well-rehearsed statement, but it was no doubt sincere. After all, when the alternative to being good was a large financial penalty, even the sleaziest bureaucrat aspires to morality.

The packet of information sent over by Jim Jones was about two inches thick, containing a number of official reports to and from the federal agency responsible for monitoring research involving human beings (as opposed to animals or laboratory specimens). Using people as guinea pigs obviously has a lot of risks involved, especially since patients who suffer from serious diseases may be desperate enough to agree to almost any kind of experimental treatment.

The research project that I had been asked to investigate was a small one. Only a group of seven patients had been assembled. Signed documents were in the file showing that all seven had been informed about the purpose of the project and what would happen during the project. All seven had agreed to participate if you can believe that signing a long legal document proves that each person knew what he or she was agreeing to.

THE ASSIGNMENT

The theory behind the project was that psychotic patients who had similar delusions should receive group therapy together rather than being mixed with patients who had different kinds of delusions. This theory flew in the face of conventional wisdom in psychiatry. Many professionals who worked with the "seriously and persistently mentally ill," as they were called, believed that having two patients with the exact same delusion in the same hospital unit was a formula for conflict. What if a person who thought he was God happened to chat with another person who thought he was God? Would they get into a fight?

The psychiatrist who dreamed up this theory, Dr. Zelicov, was a professor in the medical school. He seemed to have a strong interest in talk therapy, which was a little unusual for psychiatrists in the mid-west. The old fashioned idea of a psychiatrist meeting with his patients for hour-long weekly sessions was more often found in New York or Boston. Most modern psychiatrists concentrated on diagnosing the problem and prescribing medicines. Patients were referred to other professionals for counseling. The modern strategy was more cost-effective than the old-style approach. Besides, only very rich people could afford that much attention.

My first question was this: why had this project been approved in the first place? The number of patients was too small for serious research. There was no group of patients receiving standard care that could serve as a comparison group. And psych patients were very vulnerable to exploitation because they may not have understood what they were signing up for.

Now that I understood what the project was about I was ready to check into the complaint. The names presented in the rest of this report are entirely fictitious since it would be both illegal and unethical to reveal the identities of the people involved.

The seven people chosen to participate in the project were Miles Archer, Lew Archer, Archie Goodwin, Miss Marple, Sherlock Holmes, Archy McNally, and Dr. Watson. Miles Archer was the man who was found in the freezer. Dr. Watson was the patient who filed the complaint against Dr. Zelicov.

THE ASSIGNMENT

Watson complained that none of the patients in the project understood what the research was about. Furthermore, he said that they were tricked because none would have participated if they had known. His argument was interesting. He said that all seven of the patients were recruited because they reported seeing deceased people. They were convinced that what they saw was real, and for each of them the ability to 'see dead people' was an important though frightening gift that made them feel special. Since the purpose of the project was to find a way to cure them of seeing dead people, these folks would have refused to participate in the project had they know the plan because they did not want to be 'cured.'

As I said, this was an interesting argument. Until I spoke to the other patients, I would not know whether any agreed with Watson's point of view. Maybe the rest understood what the project was about and desired to be relieved of the stress of seeing the dead. Maybe Watson was alone in his view. Maybe he was off his meds when he wrote the complaint and forgot that he had, in good faith, agreed to participate in the project at a time when he did, indeed, desire a cure for himself.

At the time the patients were recruited into the project, all were patients in a locked hospital ward in Madison. That means they were very sick at the time since hospitals discharge patients as quickly as possible, due to the cost. After discharge, they were dispersed throughout the Madison area, except for Lew Archer. Lew Archer had been discharged to his home west of Madison, but he was already back in the locked ward. Miles Archer had been homeless; I wondered how he ended up in a freezer in Fort Atkinson. Archie Goodwin was listed as living in Happy Acres, a large group home in Janesville, which was a few miles southeast of Madison. Miss Marple lived in a smaller group home in Watertown, which was a small city north-east of Madison. Archy McNally lived in an apartment building in Milton, a city located southwest of Fort Atkinson and southeast of Madison. Sherlock Holmes was living in a homeless shelter in downtown Madison. Dr. Watson apparently lived just outside of Fort Atkinson, not more than ten minutes from my own condo.

THE ASSIGNMENT

Making appointments with most of these folks would not be possible. I would just have to drop in and ask for them, one at a time. Dr. Watson was, of course, the exception. He had provided a cell phone number, so I could call him   and   invite   myself   over.

CHAPTER 3. INTERVIEW WITH DOCTOR WATSON

Dr. Watson's address was on the outskirts of town. Watson lived in a rusty mobile home nestled into the underbrush on an overgrown lot. I steered my car into his driveway at dusk, the headlights casting flickering shadows off evergreen bushes that waved in the steady breeze despite their overcoats of snow. Thanksgiving had come and gone and winter had settled in. A storm was coming. It was the third week in December, so the temperature had dropped sharply with the disappearance of sunlight.

A rickety step led up to his front door. I knocked on it, then heard movement on the other side. A moment later, the door swung open. The man behind the door was very tall and thin, with scraggly hair and beard. He looked to be in his middle forties, though he could have been quite a bit younger but worn

out, given how difficult his life might have
been. He was dressed in a worn black suit and
narrow black tie. Incongruously, his feet were
bare. Thick black hair curled around his toes
and over the tops of his feet, which did not
look particularly clean. In fact, his whole
person emitted an odor of unwashed body and
cigarettes.

"Yeah?" he asked.

"Are you Doctor Watson?"

"That's what they call me. What do you
want?"

"I'd like to come in and talk to you for a
minute."

He didn't move so I tried again. "You
wrote a letter complaining about a research
project. I need to ask you a few questions
about it."

He grunted, then stepped back into the
room, swinging the door wide behind him. I
stepped directly into his living room, which
was carpeted with a tattered rug and stuffed
with shabby furniture. The windows were
covered with sheets of black plastic. Watson
had positioned an old metal desk in the center
of the room so that it faced a futon couch. He

waved me toward the couch and seated himself behind the desk. Picking up a well-gnawed pencil and positioning a smudged and torn scrap of paper in front of him, he glared at me from under shaggy brows and demanded, "So, what do you want to know?"

Watson leaned forward and glared at me. "There's one thing I need to know right off. Do you work for the university or the feds? Because if you work for the university, I'm not talking to you."

"The feds required the university to hire me because they see me as being an independent investigator."

"Oh yeah? What makes you trustworthy?"

"Did you hear about that business a few months ago when the university got in trouble because of its financial relationship with a big pharmaceutical company? It made a splash in the news for a couple of days. I was involved in that."

Doctor Watson leaned back in his chair. "Right. I remember that. So that was you? Good for you, man. They got what was coming to them that time." He grinned at me. "You're alright, man. You can call me Doc."

DOCTOR WATSON

Still grinning, he leaned back in his chair even further and put his feet on his desk. "Well, let me tell you my story. Several of us were on the inpatient unit over in Madison. You ever been there?"

"Nope. Never had the pleasure."

"Hah!" He laughed loudly. "Never had the pleasure! That's a good one. Some pleasure. Shoot, man. It's rotten. I mean, what else can they do when a guy is out of control? But it's still rotten." He sighed. "I've been on that unit more times than I can count. Well, maybe I could count them if they didn't dope me up with Haldol so bad that I can't remember anything afterwards. Anyway, you need to understand the situation. Several of us were there that had been in and out a bunch of times. All of us were dopey from the drugs they gave us. And," he leaned forward, "this is the most important part: we all wanted out." He swung his feet to the floor and slapped the desk with the flat of his hand. "See what I mean, man? We were all desperate to get loose from that place."

I saw his point. "You were inclined to agree to the study because you hoped they would let you out sooner if you cooperated."

"Yeah, that's sort of right. See, we all know how the system works. We've all been around. We know you can't trust anybody. And some of these crazies, they think spies are after them or something. So none of us are inclined to believe anything the white coats tell us. On the other hand, when you want out you might take a chance. You think if you show some good behavior they will think you're ready. And besides, the drugs keep you from thinking straight. See, if they came to me with some forms to sign right now, I would know it was a trick. But in there, I couldn't see the trick because my brain was fuzzy."

Doc's eyes darkened with anger, then shifted to one side and he mumbled something under his breath.

"Why did they put you in there, Doc, if you don't mind my asking?"

"I don't remember this, but they said I was tearing up a bar over in Madison."

"If that was the whole story, they would have thrown you in jail, not the psych unit. So, why the psych unit?"

He considered the question for a moment,

his eyes shifting back and forth, then replied. "You tell me."

"How would I know?"

"I bet you do."

"According to the project records, you see dead people."

"Maybe I do. You think that's impossible?"

"Heck if I know. The important question is this: did you want to stop seeing dead people when you signed the consent form?"

Doc twiddled his pencil around a little. "How would I know? I can't remember what I was thinking then. But I don't think so. Do you know why I think that?"

"Maybe because it's exciting and maybe it's the most important thing in your life. Very frightening, but important."

Doc grinned hugely. "You got it, man. Life's a drag when they put you on the Meds."

"You mean the guy behind your shoulder stops talking to you?"

Doc froze, then jumped up out of his chair. "You see a guy behind my shoulder?"

"No, I don't see anybody."

"Then you seein' inside my head, man?"

DEAD MAN IN HEAD

"No, I can't see inside your head."

"You must be, you must be," he whispered, sitting back down in his chair. He stared down at the surface of his desk for a long moment, then spoke. "Okay, I got it. You know things, too. Things other people don't know. You're one of us." He gave me a sad smile. "Okay, I know you have never been locked up for it. But you're one of us." He chuckled at the look on my face. "Don't worry, man. I won't tell the white coats. And they wouldn't believe me anyway. So you're safe from me." He stood upright and leaned over the desk toward me. "Just watch out for the dead people. They'll get you into trouble."

At this point, Doc's mouth dropped open and his eyes opened wide. "Wait a minute! You're the guy who rode the freezer down Main Street into the river. Miles Archer was in the freezer. A dead guy already got you into trouble! See, was I right or was I right? You're one of us."

This conversation had gotten way out of hand.

"Hang on, Doc. You're way off base there, but I don't want to argue about it. I'm supposed to investigate this situation and find out whether you were tricked or coerced when you signed up for that research project. Besides talking to you, I need to talk to the other people who were in the project." I pointed my finger at him. "You feel that you were coerced with the implied offer of early release. Also, you were tricked because you did not know they wanted to find a way to stop you from seeing dead people. Is that right?"

"That's right, man. You got it. It isn't right that they should trick people that way."

He shook his head. "Life's hard enough. They take away my freedom too often and in too many ways. Tricking me into research projects is too much. It goes too far. They have no right to do that. I'm a person, aren't I? I'm not some kind of wild animal they can treat however they want."

"You're right, Doc. You're a person. You have rights. You should get to live your life the way you want as long as you don't hurt anyone else."

"You got it, man! If I want to see the dead people, I have a right to do that. If I want to live here in my house with my stuff, then I have a right to do that. Of course, sometimes I act wild. Then they have to lock me up for a bit, chill me out. Otherwise, they should leave me alone."

"I see your point." And I did. His trailer looked like a dump to me. The health department would have said it was unlivable. But Doc was clearly proud of his home. There was no telling what he saw when he looked at it. If he liked it, why should my standards take precedence over his? Heck, the caves lived in by early men probably smelled bad too, and we did not say early man was insane. The cabins lived in by frontiersmen a hundred years ago were worse than this mobile home, but we did not try to lock them up for being crazy.

Or maybe we did. Maybe the reason those guys lived out in the woods was because the city folk would have thrown them in an insane asylum for living in unsanitary houses or hearing voices or even for seeing dead people. Maybe the great adventurers were all crazy by conventional standards.

"Well, that about covers it, Doc. I will try to run down the other guys tomorrow and the next day. Then I'll write up my report and we will see what the feds decide to do."

"Cool, man."

"You understand that I have not made up my mind about what I'm going to say in the report, don't you? I might agree with you and I might not."

Doc smiled. "I get it, man. You have to say that. We're cool." He chuckled, then winked at me. "Hey, man. Why don't you come back and see me after you talk to those other guys? Maybe I can explain a few things to you. Answer a few questions."

That sounded like it might be helpful. "Thanks, I'll do that."

I headed for the door. "Thanks for your time. Catch you later."

He waved from his desk. "No problem at all."

As I closed the door behind me, I heard him call out, "Watch out for those dead people!" Then he roared with laughter.

CHAPTER 4. INTERVIEW WITH LEW ARCHER

Scratch scratch scratch. Scratch scratch scratch.

It was dark in the room, but the scratching didn't worry me. It irritated me, but it didn't worry me. Bucky did this every night and being awakened at four in the morning day after day was leaving me exhausted. Usually, I would reach down beside the bed toward the floor, since Bucky always scratched the mattress on my side of the bed. Bucky would easily evade my grasp until I reached farther and farther, waking myself up even more, falling half off the bed. Then he would let me catch him and drag him by the collar up to the surface of the bed. Instead of choking and gasping, he would purr and snuggle into a warm spot.

After a week or so of this nonsense, I started taking my pillow out from under my head and swinging it down beside the bed. Bucky had no trouble evading the pillow. He would wait until I was tired of swinging at him, then start scratching again.

Betty pointed out to me that I was rewarding him with a game when what I really should have done was discourage him. She suggested I bring out the Big Gun in cat behavior modification: the spray bottle. The Big Gun was filled with plain tap water and the spray was gentle. We had purchased it from a pet store, so it was approved by all the appropriate pets' rights groups. And the darn thing was amazingly effective. The cats hated it. They would never repeat a behavior if they had been sprayed more than three times. At least, not while we were watching. I knew Bad Boy Bucky had met his match that night when I went to bed. The spray bottle was on the night stand, loaded and ready.

Four a.m. Scratch, scratch, scratch. I quickly reached up, grabbed the bottle, and sprayed myself in the face. Undeterred, I reversed the weapon and sprayed toward the sound. The scratching stopped. A shocked and offended silence arose from the direction of the floor that lasted a good thirty seconds. As I was nodding off again, I heard a tentative scratch scratch. Having kept the bottle cradled in my arms I was able to fire off a fast volley.

Bucky was cured for the evening. However, he did not jump back onto the bed and go to sleep as he should have. Instead, he galloped around the house like a small buffalo. How a fifteen-week-old kitten running on carpet could make so much noise was a mystery to me, but Bad Boy Bucky could do it. Maybe it had to do with the size of his belly, since he ate more like a pig than a cat.

Fritter never acted out as badly as Bucky did; she was a lady cat. Betty said I was biased against Bucky in favor of Fritter, but who wouldn't be? Bucky could be a real pain in the neck. Yes, I loved him. But if he woke me again, I would spray him again, relishing the revenge.

Since my sleep had been interrupted night after night for weeks, I was a bit groggy when I set out on my quest the next day. My job would be to track down as many of the research subjects as I could find and interview them. I needed my wits about me, but would have to make do without them. Thank you very much, Bucky Boy.

That morning we went through our usual routine. I got up at dawn, showered, put on the coffee, then went over to the convenience store down the street to buy a newspaper. Actually, I usually bought two papers: the Milwaukee paper and the local paper. The local paper was a lot more fun to read. Sometimes the news was a regular riot. One time they reported on a program soon to be offered at the senior center in Cambridge about weird happenings in Wisconsin. One of the weird stores was about the local werewolf. Who would have guessed that you could find one of those living in rural Wisconsin? Or that folks at a senior center would enjoy hearing about it? Rural Midwesterners have more of a sense of humor than most city people realize. It's too subtle for them to notice, but it's definitely offbeat.

This particular morning the paper carried a story about a community foundation that was soliciting grant requests. They had $500,000 to give away for projects that would improve the quality of life in our little town of Fort Atkinson. This was not a trivial amount and it made me think about ways I would spend the money if it was mine to give away. Try that exercise sometime, and you may come to the same conclusion that I reached: almost any idea I could come up with would have only a short-lived benefit. How could you spend money so that it created a long-term improvement in the lives of people in the area? I had to set that problem aside for later study.

One of my favorite sections listed coming events. The paper that morning listed a duplicate bridge club, which I was glad to see, because sometimes it seemed that the game of bridge was disappearing from the world. Bridge required more mental effort than most people wanted to exert, especially if they grew up playing video games and watching action movies.

Another scheduled event was a meeting of the local chapter of the national alliance for the mentally ill. City people might think that all mentally ill folks lived in urban areas, but this was not accurate. One time the local paper carried a matter of fact story about a police call involving a man who complained that the voices in his head had gotten so loud that he could not hear anything else. The paper reported that the man's girlfriend had arrived on the scene and promised to take him to the emergency room for more meds. Rural emergency rooms saw their share of mentally ill people who had slipped off their trolleys a little bit.

Seventeen events were listed as occurring over the next two days. Interestingly, four were meetings of Alcoholics Anonymous groups and two were Weight Watchers groups. In fact, the state of Wisconsin was reporting a record number of arrests for drunk driving. It was obvious that local people were quietly struggling with their share of personal demons.

The thought of demons reminded me that I was due to get out of my chair and visit some people who had some serious demons to fight. My first stop was the hospital where Lew Archer was staying on a locked ward. The roads were icy and I didn't dare go faster than forty miles per hour. Everyone else was passing me. One turkey honked as he went by. I understood his irritation, but I was doing my best.

It was late in the morning when I checked in at the desk on the first floor of the building that housed the psychiatric patients. The locked ward was on the fourth floor and, naturally enough, visitors were not allowed in unless they had a reason to be there. Jim Jones, the vice president for research, had provided me with a letter signed by the chair of the psychiatry department that granted me access. Even so, the clerk at the front desk was cautious enough to confer by telephone with her counterparts on the unit before letting me pass by her. I gave her high marks for taking her job seriously.

The elevator took me to the fourth floor, then disgorged me into a hallway with no signs telling me which direction led to the locked wing. Wandering around brought me up against a door that blocked off the hallway into the unit. The windows were darkened so I could not see all the way in, but no one appeared to be directly on the other side. I pushed a button labeled 'talk' and called out 'hello?' After about twenty seconds, a voice responded, "Yes? May I help you?"

"I'm here to see Lew Archer."

"Visiting hours are this afternoon, sir."

"I have special permission for this visit."

Silence.

"This visit is not personal. It's official business."

There was a long silence. I assumed the person guarding this door had not yet been told about my impending arrival. Eventually a buzzer sounded, so I pushed on the door and it opened into a dimly lit hallway. The nurses' desk was about thirty feet down the corridor on the left. A few patient rooms were on the right side, but they were empty. Presumably the patients were in the day room.

I signed in at the nurses' desk, where a heavy-set, muscular man in white pants and a tee-shirt was busy filling out forms. The aide told me to wait while he went to get Lew Archer. He must have only gone a few feet, because the two of them were back in a few seconds. Lew was a big man, with skin as dark as it can get, who must have weighed close to three hundred pounds. He was wearing what looked like thrift store clothes and had a slow shuffling gait.

"You have a visitor, Lew," said the aide in a loud voice.

Lew looked at me blankly, but said nothing.

"You can go into the interview room," the aide told me, gesturing toward a room behind the nurses' station. He took Archer's arm and led us both into the room. As he left us, the aide said if I needed anything to 'just ask,' then closed the door.

Archer and I sat there quietly for a moment, then I introduced myself and told him why I was there. Archer said nothing in response, so I tried again.

"Lew, did you know you signed up for a research project a few months ago?"

After shifting in his seat, he replied in a deep, slow voice, "I did?"

"Yes, you did. A group of people who were staying on this floor all signed up to be in a special group. You were in the group."

Lew looked confused.

"Doc Watson was in the group, Miles Archer, and some others. Do you remember now?"

"Oh yeah. That group." He gave me a slow smile. I wasn't sure whether he remembered the group or not.

Lew smiled at me at this point. "Can I get out of here now?" he asked.

This question threw me off balance. "That isn't my decision, Lew." He just stared at me, waiting. I tried a different tack, which proved to be a mistake. "Lew, you must be in here because people were worried that you might get hurt out on the street, right?"

Lew's smile turned cynical. "You sayin' that safety is more important than freedom?" he asked.

"Sometimes."

His smile broadened. "Then let's you and me change clothes. You can be in here where it's safe and I'll go out and take my chances on the street."

I didn't answer; he knew I wasn't going to take him up on his offer.

He leaned back in his chair, eyelids drooping. "You a fool, man. Got no time for fools." He appeared to be dropping off to sleep. In the moment of silence that followed, we could hear shouting and laughing echoing from outside the room. The background noise was eerie. Then the door opened and a matronly black woman entered the room. She was carefully dressed, her hair was nicely done, and she was not wearing white. She did not look at all like the staff members I had seen up to this point.

"Lew," she said. "I need to get your signature on some forms."

"Hey, Mama," he responded, "you gonna get me outta here?"

"Yes, dear," she said soothingly. "Soon. When it's time."

"I'll get my bag," he said, starting to rise.

"No, no, not yet," she responded, putting her hand on his shoulder and pushing him back down into his chair. "Just sign these forms for the nurses." She pushed the forms in front of him and held out a pen.

Lew pushed them away and ignored the pen. "I don't wanna sign no forms."

"Why not, Lew honey?"

"Don't know what they for. Could be anything."

She sighed. Obviously this conversation was going about as she had expected. She pulled the forms over to her side of the table, sat down, and started to sign them herself. She had beautiful handwriting, very clear and firm.

I leaned over to look at what she was doing. She was writing "Lewis Archer" on each form. She shot me a suspicious but defiant glare. "You must be a school teacher," I said. "Your cursive looks like you've been practicing it for a long time."

"Thank you," she said. "And yes, I have been teaching K through 12 for thirty years." She finished the stack of forms and turned toward me. "Now, what business do you have with my son?"

"I'm auditing a research project Lew was enrolled in. I needed to ask him a few questions about it."

"Did he give you the information you needed?"

"Not really. He does not seem to remember much about it."

"That's no surprise."

"Maybe you could tell me about it. I'll buy you a coffee or a soda. Are you available any time soon?"

"Yes, as soon as I turn these forms in at the desk." She stood up to go.

Lew looked up. "Can I go now, Mama?"

"No, dear, not just yet. You just rest while everybody does their paperwork. You know the paper comes first."

"Yeah, I know," he said resignedly. We left him sitting in his chair. After we went through the locked door in the corridor, she led me back to the elevators, then turned to me with an outstretched hand. "Margaret Archer," she said. "Ed Schumacher," I responded, bowing slightly as I shook her hand. Her eyes crinkled a bit at the corners as she suppressed a smile. We rode down to the ground floor in silence. A few chairs formed a waiting room outside the reception area. It was empty at that moment. Margaret showed me the coffee vending machine, located behind the elevators. We punched in our selections then seated ourselves in a couple of vinylclad aluminum-framed chairs.

After we were comfortable, Margaret fixed me with a direct stare and waited for me to explain myself.

"Well, it's like this," I began. "I can't give you all of the particulars, but the main issue you might be interested in is simply this: Lew was enrolled in a research project that involved a small group of people who all happened to be upstairs on the locked unit at the same time. They also all had similar delusions."

"Yes," Margaret said. "I remember that. What about it?"

"The federal agency that monitors research directed the university to contract with an independent investigator to audit the project. That's me. My job is to find out if all the important procedures were followed."

"There has to be more to the story than that," Margaret said. "Random checks I can understand, but bringing in an outside investigator can't be routine." She was a smart woman.

"You might have a point there, but if you don't mind, let's just skip ahead to the essential facts as they relate to Lew. First, you have already confirmed that Lew was in the project. Do you think he knew what he was signing up for?" I gave her the most wide-eyed and guileless facial expression I could muster up.

She was not fooled one bit.

"You mean, did I sign the consent form for him."

"Did you?"

"Why would I want to admit to such a thing?"

"Maybe I should just pull out the form and see if the handwriting is as beautiful as yours."

Margaret laughed. "Yes, I imagine that could prove something. Lew writes like a ten year old. But what difference does it make anyway?"

"Nobody is supposed to be enrolled in a research project unless he knows what it's about and has agreed to be in it."

"Lew gave me his power of attorney years ago. I am his guardian and the payee on his disability checks. Besides that, I'm his mother, and since his judgment is impaired, I have to make choices for him."

"Even children have to agree to be in a research project. Their parents can't just sign them up without talking them into it."

"That's ridiculous. Look, you don't understand how it is with mentally ill people. The medical care system is a mess when it comes to people with chronic mental illness. Unless parents get deeply involved and push hard, the patients won't get what they need."

"So I've heard." She looked at me with some suspicion in her gaze. "There's a lot of truth in what you say."

"It's completely true. Anyone who has had a family member in the system knows how quickly they get dumped on the street with no services. And dumping them is easy since the sick person often does not want any services. They just want to be let out the door."

"Like Lew."

"Yes, like Lew. He just wants out now. He's not thinking about where he will sleep or where he will get his next meal. He definitely is not thinking about where he will get his meds. Without those meds he will be back in the emergency room in less than a month, if he hasn't been killed in a fight before then." She was breathing hard from her passionate outburst. At the same time, it sounded well-rehearsed.

"I understand the problem."

"I don't think you do. The system gives an insane person rights that he can't handle, then makes me break the rules if I want him to get services. Yes, I sign his name. Yes, I make sure the doctor gets all the information he should have about Lew, even if the doctor doesn't want to take the time to talk to me. I have to fight and fight and fight to get anything out of this system. People like Lew need to be placed in supervised apartments. They can't be just dumped out on the street. Families that give up the fight against the system get nothing that they need." She was really steamed.

"Believe me, I understand what you are trying to do. Still, the law says Lew has rights. If the law needs to be changed, then our society should change it. "

"While we wait for that to happen, Lew and thousands of other people like him could die of exposure or violence." She stopped talking and the silence between us began to stretch uncomfortably.

"Margaret," I said finally, "upstairs when Lew asked me to let him out I mentioned safety and he asked me if I preferred safety to freedom. That made me think about what I would prefer if I was the one locked up. Would I want to be able to make my own choices, even if my judgment was impaired?" I took a swig of my cold coffee. "Sure I would. I do it all the time. We live in a complicated world. Most of my important decisions are based on guesses about what might work out best. When you go to the polls, do you really know that you are voting for a candidate who will do a good job? When you park your retirement money somewhere, are you sure it's a going to be a good investment? We make choices and sometimes we guess wrong."

"It doesn't usually make us homeless or hungry when we make a bad choice," Margaret said through clenched teeth. "We aren't likely to choose to take a ten mile walk in the snow, barefoot and hatless."

"That's true. But I have to tell you, the older I get the more I realize that life is tragic. Everybody gets sick and dies, some sooner than others. It's part of the Grand Plan, whether we like it or not."

Margaret was done with me by this point. She got up and went out the door without another word, throwing her full cup of coffee into the trash as she went. She was angry, and who could blame her; life had dealt her a nasty hand of cards. She was left holding two's and three's when she needed aces to protect her son. Unfortunately, even if she had all the aces, there was no way to protect her son from all the dangers he faced. Lew was a very vulnerable guy, despite his enormous size and obvious physical strength.

As I left the hospital, I was mulling over the problem faced by the families of mentally ill people. If you advocate strongly on behalf of your loved one and you succeed in forcing the system to provide services, will the patient be happier than he would have been if you had left him alone? And what kind of ethical boundaries do you have to cross to be a 'strong advocate?' When you fraudulently sign the patient's name to a form, you have crossed a line. When you exaggerate the patient's symptoms to the doctor so that he will crank up the meds, what kind of harm might you be doing? When you tell the patient where to live and how to live, you have imposed your values and preferences on someone who sees the world through an entirely different lens. Is all this to make the patient happier? Or is it really intended to make the parent feel better about the tragedy of mental illness?

To the uninitiated, the guilt felt by the parent of a mentally ill person is hard to imagine. Modern science knows that unless you tortured your child, you probably did not cause his psychosis. Even so, parents feel that the way the child 'turned out' reflects on their parenting. And when living in the same home with an adult psychotic turns out to be an unacceptable and unsustainable option, the parent gets a double dose of guilt because many other parents simply do not understand why the sick person cannot just live at home.

Of course, many parents make that sacrifice. But, unless one person stays at home all day on guard, drug dealers or a crowd of other undesirables are likely to end up in their living room, eating their food, and stealing their television. A shadowy crowd of low-lifes make their living by exploiting the mentally disabled. When the monthly disability check arrives, the creeps come out of their dark corners and buddy up to – or beat up - the people who should be benefiting from those checks. Unless we intend to lock up all the mentally disabled people in the world for their own protection, someone will find a way to periodically exploit them.

The tragedy of mental illness does not just affect the sick person. It affects the mental health of their families as well. A person with a serious and persistent mental illness is often fated to live a dangerous life. Parents are forced to observe, to help a little when they can, but mostly they just watch. Parents of mentally ill persons face a double-whammy when it comes to emotions: guilt and powerlessness, both of which are very hard to bear.

The interviews with Lew and Margaret Archer gave me a lot to think about. I drove home at a sedate pace, then parked myself in the garage to smoke my pipe. Smoking in the house was a bad idea, but smoking outside in December was not a pleasant experience. Consequently, I had placed a chair, a space heater, and a side table in a corner of the garage. With a warm coat and hat, I could relax and consider the complexities of modern life for as much as an hour at a time before becoming chilled.

After returning from the psych hospital, I

zeroed in on my smoking spot like a homing pigeon. The ethical dilemmas facing parents had no simple answer, so I gave up on that issue. Instead, my mind turned to the mysterious circumstances of the dead man in the freezer. Each of the patients in the research project had at least one dead man in the head. How did imaginary dead people produce an actual dead person? Not being an expert on the occult, I was pretty sure that dead people did not directly cause the death of real people. Maybe this would sound like an unenlightened attitude to some. After all, Hamlet said there are more things in heaven and earth than were dreamed of in Horatio's philosophy. He said that because he was in dialogue with a ghost.

Despite the possibility that ghosts might exist, I was going to attack this mystery scientifically. I was going to assume that the dead cannot reach through the veil of tears and crush the life out of us. Perhaps that sort of thing could actually happen, but it had to be so rare that it should be ignored as a possible explanation for the death of a particular person, i.e., Miles Archer.

DEAD MAN IN HEAD

Shaking off the chill, I returned to the basic challenge of any person who plays detective: asking the right questions. In this case, the key question on the table appeared to be the following: was Miles Archer's death connected to the research project? If so, who killed him and why?

The news reports after the body was found in the freezer had said little about the circumstances of the death. Apparently, the outrageous way the body had been discovered was more newsworthy. They reported the victim's name, that he was homeless, and that he had apparently ingested a large quantity of alcohol prior to death. Very little else was known. My investigation of the research project had turned up more background on the victim than the reporter had found.

Assuming for the moment that Archer's death was connected to the project, my list of suspects was limited. It included the other patients who had been in the group and the researcher, Dr. Zelicov. I was willing to rule out Lew Archer, despite his history of violence, because he had been locked up too much of the time and because the placement of the body in a freezer seemed to require far more subtlety than Lew could display.

The most obvious suspect for the murder was the man who had been pushing the freezer. Nevertheless, to assume that someone had killed a man, placed the body in a freezer, then pushed the freezer down the middle of Main Street was jumping to conclusions. That would lack discretion, if you know what I mean. You would have to be nuts to do that. For now, I was willing to accept the working hypothesis that the man pushing the freezer was not the killer. Sometimes the most obvious answer is the correct one, but I intended to keep an open mind on the subject.

After finishing my pipe, I went upstairs where I found Betty reading a book.

"How is your day going?" she asked.

"Just fine. Interesting. This investigation of the psych research project has some fascinating ethical twists and turns."

"That's nice. I'm glad you are working on a project." Betty did not have much interest in the projects that I got involved in, but she generally liked to see me busy. She knew I was the sort of person who had to work to avoid getting depressed. And she also knew that, once drawn into a puzzle, I would give it my full attention until it was solved. Obsessive and compulsive were two of my more prominent traits.

Walking into the spare bedroom where we kept the computer, I turned it on and waited for a connection. It was time to check for messages and pay a few bills. Fritter came in, jumped on my lap for a little petting, then moved to her favorite spot: the modem. The modem was warm and also was under the desk lamp. By sitting there, Fritter was warmed from above and below, which she really seemed to enjoy. She would sit there for hours if I was working on the computer. Bucky came in next, attempted to jump on my lap, fell off, and had to be picked up. He immediately rolled onto his side and began purring. When I tired of petting him and began working on the computer, he sat on the table and watched me. When I lifted my hand to move the mouse, his head would turn to follow the action. Fritter's did as well. The two cat heads moved in synchrony: forward, back, left, right. This went on until I stopped noticing them. The fascination with my computer work was unfathomable, who could know what a cat was thinking? Their mysterious nature was part of the reason humans loved having them around.

Betty came in after half an hour or so. She was wearing an unfortunate black dress.

"How do you like my new dress?" she asked. "I just bought it."

"Mmhmph" I said to buy time. Every husband knew when he was in a dangerous situation. He knew it because he had erred on the side of honesty early in the marriage and still bore the scars.

"What does that mean?"

"Very nice." Okay, so it was an outright lie. But when dealing with women's fashion, the normal rules of ethical behavior simply do not apply.

"Do you think it's too tight?"

Darn, a direct question. "Your butt never looked smaller." This was the stock answer. Trial and error had revealed that it was always acceptable.

Betty turned to look at her behind. She considered it's magnitude for a moment, then asked, "should I wear it to the holiday dinner with the clinic staff?"

At this point, some courage on my part was required. If she wore that thing to the dinner, she would decide halfway through the meal that it was too tight.

"That other one you have is better."

"Which other one?"

"You know, the one I like."

"Which one do you like?"

"The one with a belt. It shows you have a waist. And makes your bodice more prominent."

"Bodice? What have you been reading?"

"Bodice is a real word."

"Maybe it was a hundred years ago. You should get out more." Then she whirled around and left the room. In five minutes she was back, wearing a looser dress that was longer, had more color, had a belt, and displayed her charms admirably, both of them.

"I decided this would be better," she announced.

"It's great. It makes you look like Barbara Streisand."

"Why do you think Barbara Streisand looks good?"

"Because she looks like you. By the way, Andrew and I are going out for a beer tomorrow night." Andrew was Betty's cousin. He lived in Fort Atkinson, also.

"You're impossible" she declared, then left. Sometimes a stupid remark combined with a change of subject is the best strategy for ending a conversation. Try it sometime. See if it   doesn't   work

CHAPTER 5. INTERVIEW WITH ARCHIE GOODWIN

The next day I was eager to get back to work on my investigation. My first task of the day was a visit to Archie Goodwin who lived in a group home called Happy View in Janesville, near Madison. Janesville was only about half an hour away, down Highway 26. When I drove up to the building, I was surprised to see that it was very large. It obviously had begun its life as an apartment building or hotel. It must have contained several hundred rooms.

The sidewalk out front and up the street in both directions was dotted with people who looked like they might be residents of Happy View. Many had an air of unkemptness, with shabby clothes and hair in disarray. Buildings in nearby strip malls were boarded up. It appeared that being near Happy View was not an attractive location for businesses.

A crowd of people were standing around the reception desk joking among themselves. At first I could not distinguish the residents from the staff. However, it gradually became apparent who was more alert, so I guessed they must be the people in charge. On the other hand, I may have guessed wrong.

Archie Goodwin's name was called repeatedly. His room was called via telephone and the day room received the benefit of several loud shouts. Eventually, somebody found Archie out on the patio. He approached me with some caution, but when I suggested driving over to the Dairy Queen he quickly signed himself out and away we went.

Archie did not ask why I was visiting him. He just waited quietly until he got his Blizzard, then dug into it with enthusiasm. That fellow really knew how to enjoy his ice cream. He seemed to forget everything going on around him as he consumed it. Finally, he set aside the empty cup with a sigh and leaned back in the seat.

Archie was a young man, probably in his

twenties. He was skinny, boney even, with hollow cheeks. He looked as if he had been seriously malnourished at some time in his life.

I decided to try an indirect opening. "Say, Archie, what's it like living in that place?"

Archie looked at me with amazement. "How do you think? How would you like to live with a bunch of crazies? Those people are nuts. Ain't a soul there I would hang out with if I had a choice. Wish I could get outa there. But they ain't never letting me out. It's like a prison."

"Why can't you get out? They let you sign out with no problem."

"Yeah, I could walk away. Lots of people do that. But I don't have no job. Nobody is going to hire me. With no job I can't get a place to live. Can't get no car so can't drive to a job, anyway. I'm trapped, man."

At this point he turned to me and asked, "who are you? And why did you buy me an ice cream?"

"My name is Ed. I need to ask you some questions about a research project you were in back when you were on the inpatient unit at the psych hospital. And I'm sure glad I bought you that ice cream because it's been years since I saw anybody enjoy one as much as you did."

Archie snorted. He obviously thought I was scamming him. "What research project are you talking about? I wasn't in no research project."

"It was like a therapy group. Doc Watson, Sherlock Holmes, Lew Archer, and some others were in the group with you."

"I remember some of those guys. That was research? I thought it was just another damn boring group thing. They made us do groups every day."

"Would you have said 'no' if they asked you to be in a group for research?"

"Damn right. Groups are a drag." He hesitated for a moment, then asked, "What did we talk about in the group? Sometimes groups can be fun. Were there any women in the group?"

"Yes, there was a woman in the group-- Miss Marple."

"Marple! She was hot. But way off in the 'zone, if you know what I mean. What did we talk about in the group?"

"You talked about seeing dead people."

Archie froze. "No way," he said.

"Yes, that was what the research was about."

"They was researching our dead people?"

"Uh, no, they were trying to figure out how to help you stop seeing them."

Archie was silent for a moment. Finally he said, "no way."

"Would you have signed up if you knew that was what they were trying to do?"

Silence. Then, "I'm ready to go back now."

We drove back to the group home without talking. I pulled up in front of the place and, as he started to get out of the car, I stopped him with a question. "Archie, did it work?"

Archie stared at me with his big starvation eyes dominating his skinny face. "What do you think, man? How in the hell would talking in a group keep dead people away? That's just stupid." He slammed the door and slouched away.

Goodwin certainly had a point. The whole premise of the research project seemed ridiculous. Had the investigator really believed this treatment was going to work? Who could be that dumb?

ARCHIE GOODWIN

As I drove back to Fort Atkinson, I remembered that I was supposed to meet Andrew for a beer. We generally met at Sal's, since that was convenient for both of us. Come to think of it, no place in Fort was more than ten minutes away from where either of us lived.

Going directly to Sal's parking lot, rather than stopping off at home first, I found that Andrew was already at a table, nursing a beer.

"Hey, how's it going?" he asked.

"Just fine. Been here long?"

"About five minutes."

After ordering a Miller for myself, we talked about the weather a bit, then Andrew asked me, "so, Betty tells me you've got yourself a new case."

"Yep. Sure do."

"How did that happen?"

"The med school in Madison called me and asked me to look into something for them."

"I thought you and them weren't on the best of terms."

"Well, you can sure say that again. But it turns out the feds told them they should call me in. An independent perspective was needed."

"Why independent?"

"Because the feds knew those guys at the med school would cook their investigation till it came out right if they had a chance."

We both chuckled at that for a bit.

"Well, are you turning up anything interesting?" Andrew was an investigator for the state of Wisconsin. He found my little amateur investigations amusing.

"For sure. Somehow it's tied up with the dead guy in the freezer."

"The one you rode into the river?"

"Yup. The dead guy was one of the patients in the research project. The feds suspect that the death may have somehow been due to the project. That tells me that if I can figure out how the two are connected, I might solve the murder case."

"You can't investigate a murder. You're not qualified and you have no legal standing."

"True. But I'm not investigating the murder. I'm investigating the research project. It's not my fault that the two are connected."

"How could they be connected?"

"I don't know. I was hoping you could give me some ideas. The facts are pretty skimpy at this point. All the people in the research project are mentally ill, including the dead guy."

'Mentally ill? What's wrong with them?"

"Psychosis. They have some serious delusions. They see dead people."

"You're trying to get at the truth by interviewing these people?"

"Yup."

"Well, good luck. And you better stay away from the murder issue. You'll get into big trouble." Andrew sighed, then relented a bit. "I don't have any ideas for you. When you get more information, let's talk about it again. Maybe something will come out later. What else are you learning?"

"The way our society deals with people who have serious mental problems is really shameful. I say it's shameful because of the way it turns out, but I don't really have a clear idea of how to do it better."

"What do you mean?"

"Well, these folks have trouble coping. It's not their fault; they just don't understand the world the same way everyone else does. In some ways they just don't get it. In other ways, they understand their situation very well, but still can't manage to cope very well. We seem to be telling them just to go out and get a job and work hard and everything will be fine. But not everyone can do that. As a last resort, we give them a disability check, but that doesn't solve all the problems. It's a mess."

"What's wrong with just giving them a check?"

"Well, for one thing, the cost of living is quite a bit more than a disability check will cover. Until we find ways to keep the cost of living down, lot's of people, not just psych patients, will continue to be deep in poverty, not able to afford basic food and medicine and housing."

"Oh, this is where you say everyone should drive electric bikes." Andrew liked to tease me about the time I got into selling electric bicycle motors.

"An electric bike sure would be a form of cheap transportation. It's environmentally safe and it's affordable."

"Well, I see your point," Andrew said.

"But the price of gas has gone up and now renewable energy sources are going to be used a lot more. That should make you happy."

"Happy? You must be kidding. These days it seems that everyone is on the renewable energy bandwagon. Rising oil prices have created the impetus, and a variety of businesses and governments have experienced suspiciously sudden conversions to the Green camp. It looks to me like the political support for energy conservation is rapidly being diverted into profits for business interests rather than lower energy costs and a lower cost of living for consumers."

"Do you really believe that? Give me a for instance."

"Okay, think about this. In Northern Ireland the government plans to develop a Renewable Energy Strategy. The Ulster Farmers' Union praised the decision, pointing out that their members are happy to grow the crops. A boom in the local agriculture industry appears imminent, at taxpayers' expense."

"Farm subsidies are pretty popular around here. You better be careful what you say against them."

DEAD MAN IN HEAD

By this time I was on a roll. "Even the garbage business is getting in on the gravy train. In Malaysia, the Jana landfill, located 40km outside of Kuala Lumpur, is one of the city's main municipal storage waste sites. Landfills are a potential source of 'free fuel' that would otherwise be flared or vented. This sounds like a good opportunity for tax payer savings, but we shouldn't jump to conclusions about who will benefit. GE built the plant and opened it in 2004 before the current oil price hike, presumably because they anticipated a profit. The government of Malaysia has been giving a 70 percent tax break for five years to companies that develop renewable energy sources. They now are proposing to increase the tax break to 100 percent and extend it for ten years. How can the cost of living be reduced for the average consumer when business is getting deals like that?"

"Okay, maybe our utility bills won't go down. But hybrid cars are available now and they reduce how much the average consumer pays for gas."

"Yeah, right, hybrid cars. What a crock. Hybrid vehicles are not affordable for working class families."

"Not affordable?"

"Right. The last car you bought was a Dodge Neon. A hybrid would have cost you more than twice as much. The savings at the pump will never be enough to make up for the higher price of the car. Besides, low income people can't come up with the monthly payments for an expensive car, no matter how good their mileage is."

"Are you trying to say that the renewable energy policies are all cooked up by corporations so they can increase their profits?"

"Many of these policies will benefit businesses more than consumers. Here is another example for you. The state of Connecticut is 'incentivizing' businesses to use renewable energy sources such as fuel cells or solar panels. Millions in grants are available for businesses to set up such renewable energy generating facilities at their sites. Taxpayers are paying the bill for these changes. A tax on businesses that refused to switch to renewable energy sources would have had the same effect, at less cost to the taxpayer."

DEAD MAN IN HEAD

"Where do you get these stories? They sound pretty outlandish to me."

"Off the internet, of course. I just do a Google news search and it pulls up the newspaper stories." I took a sip from my beer, then went on. "Try this one. In Washington State, Puget Sound Energy has acquired 100 percent ownership of a big wind energy project. The CEO of the company had the gall to praise the hard work of local and state officials who made this monopoly possible for his company. He didn't explain why local ownership of smaller wind energy generating sites wouldn't have been better for the people of the state of Washington."

"Okay, that one sounds a little out there. I'll give you one."

"Let me try for another. The governor of Georgia said the devastation caused by recent hurricanes had motivated him to push his state toward greater 'energy security.' This was smart. He managed to bring up the words 'security' and 'disaster' in the same sentence. Anyway, he wants to give tax credits and incentives for people who drive fuel-efficient cars, homeowners who convert to solar power, and businesses that create new forms of energy. Unfortunately, the governor did not say how the people who lost their jobs and homes due to hurricanes would benefit from the tax credits. With no jobs they won't be paying taxes."

"Okay, one more point for you. Betcha can't get another."

"Bet I can. Try this. The governor of Vermont said big industrial wind energy factories with tall turbines 'don't belong' on Vermont's mountaintops. But, at the same time, he is supporting a commercial wind project to be placed on top of a mountain that will include four 330-foot tall strobe-lighted turbines located on government land. He says he is not being inconsistent because the project is just a demonstration project. It sounds to me like government land is being provided so that big business can get the kinks out of industrial wind technology. Once again, the taxpayers foot the bill so commercial interests can cash in on the energy crisis. What will the little guy get out of it?"

"You sound more like a socialist every day." Andrew said.

DEAD MAN IN HEAD

"When you are retired and trying to live on a social security check, you will wish the cost of living was lower. And if you or one of your kids develops a serious mental illness and can't figure out how to keep a check book, I might just tell you to go out and buy a hybrid car. You remember what Marie Antoinette said when she was told the peasants were starving?"

"Yup. She said 'let them eat cake.'"

"Here's to cake," I said, raising my glass. Andrew raised his in response, we clinked them together, and drank them down.

CHAPTER 6. INTERVIEW WITH MISS MARPLE

Bucky was being his usual self that morning, bounding around like mad, clawing my wool slacks, clawing my office chair, and pulling my ties off the hanger onto the floor. I didn't mind because this was the day Bucky went in to be neutered. How often do we get to behave in a socially responsible manner and also get revenge at the same time? Don't get me wrong; I loved Bucky, but I was still gleeful about having his goods snipped off.

I picked him up to pet him, then popped him into his carrying bag. Betty was worried, of course. She thought he might die under the knife.

"Poor guy. Don't you feel bad for him?"

"Not really."

"He might die during the operation."

"He won't die during the operation."

"He might. It happens."

"He's young and very healthy. He'll be fine." After that exchange I hustled him out the door. When we were ushered into the vets examination room, Bucky was his usual, lovable self. He purred so much that the vet had trouble listening to his heart and lungs. The vet and her assistant loved him.

"He is very friendly, isn't he?"

"Yes indeed. He loves everybody. Say, do you think he will be a little less rambunctious after the operation?"

The vet shook her head, "No, I'm afraid not. Would you like more information about the procedure?"

"I'd rather not know the details, frankly." The vet and her assistant found my squeamishness amusing. They said I could pick him up anytime after noon. "Oh, one more thing."

The vet had been on her way through the door. She stopped with a quizzical expression. "Yes?" she asked.

"This is kind of a big event. My wife is nervous about the operation." I hesitated, unsure about how to go on. "Yes, Mr. Schumacher?" the vet asked.

"Could you save the parts for us?" I blurted out.

"Excuse me?"

"Well, you know, old people like to show their scars after a big surgery and when you pay a lot of money to have your car fixed they offer to give you the old parts, so I put those two ideas together and thought I would just ask for Bucky's parts."

The vet thought for a moment. "I can't think of any reason why not," she said, then left the room shaking her head at the strangeness of customers.

The next stop after the vet clinic was a small group home in Watertown, which was located about 45 minutes north of Fort Atkinson on Highway 26. This was where I had been told I could find Miss Marple. The drive over took less than an hour, but then I got turned around, as I usually do, and wasted nearly an hour trying to find the address. It turned out to be an ordinary looking house in a residential neighborhood. The streets were lined with trees, leaves were mixed in with snow on the ground, and toys were laying abandoned on the drifts.

DEAD MAN IN HEAD

I parked on the street in front of the house, then climbed the steps to the front door. Ringing the bell brought a heavyset man to the door. When I explained my errand, he acted as if he had not been told that I had a legitimate reason for talking to Miss Marple. On the other hand, he did not appear to care one way or the other. He led me into the living room, where an attractive young black woman sat in an easy chair with an afgan covering her lap and legs. My escort did not introduce us. He just waved me toward her, then left the room.

"Hi. My name is Ed," I said. "Do you mind if I ask you a few questions?"

Miss Marple did not answer, but she favored me with an angelic smile. I took that as permission to charge ahead.

"A few weeks ago when you were in the hospital you were part of a research project. Do you remember that?"

"Maybe," she said still smiling.

"Some of the other people in the group were Doc Watson, Lew Archer, and Miles Archer. Do you remember those guys?"

"Maybe."

"Can you tell me anything about the group you were in?"

Miss Marple hesitated, then said, "I've been sick."

That was when the realization finally struck me: she had no idea what I was talking about. The smile was angelic, but the mind was vacant. As we used to say back home, the lights were on but nobody was home. There was no point in asking any more questions. I found the heavy set man in the kitchen and told him I was leaving. He didn't seem surprised at the brevity of my visit. He also didn't seem to care.

CHAPTER 7. INTERVIEW WITH SHERLOCK HOLMES

I went directly from Miss Marple's place to see the last person on my list, Sherlock Holmes, who was reputed to be living in a homeless shelter in downtown Madison. The place was not hard to find, being a large and relatively new building on one of the main streets. Inside the front door, visitors were confronted with a receptionist who sat in a glassed-in enclosure. I wondered if the glass was bullet-proof. Down the corridor behind her, I could see a large room walled off into sections with what looked like floor-to-ceiling chain link fencing. Living there would be like living in a dog kennel, I thought.

When I asked for Holmes, I was told that he did not reside there anymore. The receptionist suggested I try another shelter, just down the street. The other shelter was called "Saint Martha's Mission."

SHERLOCK HOLMES

When I found the place I realized that not all homeless shelters are equal. Holmes definitely had taken a step down when he moved to this place. It was a large building that was in poor repair. Scruffy men were hanging out around it, leaning against the building smoking cigarettes. It reminded me of the large group home where I had found Archie Goodwin. Perhaps the only difference between the two was that Archie was given medicine in Happy View while Saint Martha's had no health services. Yet, when I stepped in the front door I quickly reached the conclusion that a lot of the residents could have benefited from some pysch meds. One man was dressed in a bed sheet and had a trash can on his head. Much of the conversation that could be overheard seemed to make no sense at all.

They found Holmes for me. That was when I received the biggest surprise of the day. Sherlock Holmes was the man with the freezer. He was the man whom I had helped, much to my detriment. He had abandoned me to the police when the freezer ended up in the river. And he definitely had some explaining to do, starting with the biggest question now on my mind: how did Miles Archer's body get into the freezer?

When he got in the car, Holmes asked me for a cigarette. When told I had none, he became even more withdrawn, so I pulled over behind a convenience store and gave him some money go in and buy a pack. He scooted out in a hurry. While he was gone, I called Betty on my cell phone to tell her where I was and how long it would be before I came home.

During the call, I got out of the car and leaned against the driver's side door. Holmes returned, with a lighted cigarette in his hand. I told him "just a minute" and turned away to finish the call. He needed time to finish his cigarette, anyway. I did not want him to smoke in the car.

Five minutes later we were driving away. We quickly became entangled in traffic, however. All the cars on the street froze in place as a fire truck and a couple of police cars rushed past us with sirens blaring. After they were gone, traffic resumed its flow. Holmes and I ended up at a Wendy's, with me having a bowl of chili and him having a large value meal. He was vacuuming up his food like a ravenous Hoover when we first seated ourselves, so I said nothing until he finished. Then, I went through my spiel about what I was trying to learn and why I was talking to him.

"Do you remember the group sessions, Holmes?" I asked him.

"Yeah. Sorta."

"Did you know you had signed up for a research project?"

"Yeah. I guess so. It didn't matter. Something to do."

"Did you know what the project was trying to do?"

"Maybe I did at the time. Don't remember. It wouldn't have made any difference to me. I still would have signed up."

"Why wouldn't the purpose of the project make any difference to you?"

"You say they were trying to stop us from seeing dead people by having a group? That's dumber'n dirt, man. Waste of time. But what the hell; wasting time is all you got to do when you're in the psych unit."

"Well, that's great. You gave me the information I needed." Now it was time to

DEAD MAN IN HEAD

change to a more interesting subject.

"Holmes, we've seen each other before, you know."

'Yeah?" His eyes became hooded and cautious.

"Yep. When you were pushing that freezer across Main Street in Fort Atkinson, I stopped to help. Remember that?"

"What about it?"

"What about it? You left me in the lurch there, fellah. The freezer ended up in the river, with me going along with it."

Holmes chuckled at that image.

"Yeah, you might think that sounds funny. But after they dragged me out of the water, the cops found a body in that freezer. They had a lot of questions I couldn't answer, like who put the body in the freezer? I wish you had been there to explain things a bit."

"Don't like cops. So I split."

"Well, at least you can tell me what was going on. The dead guy was Miles Archer. He was in your research group. Somebody killed him by sticking him in a freezer when he was loaded and letting him suffocate or freeze to death or maybe both. Who did that and why?

"He asked for it," Holmes blurted out.

I was stunned into silence for a moment. My mouth hung open. Had Holmes just said what I thought he said? It came close to an admission of guilt.

"Are you telling me..." I started to ask him, but it was too late. He was out of his seat and through the door before I could finish the question. He was moving fast, so I didn't bother to try to catch up with him. He did not appear to want to discuss the subject any further.

With my interview terminated so abruptly, there was nothing to do except go home. I picked Bucky up at the vet and took him back to the condo. He didn't seem to be particularly uncomfortable. Then I smoked my pipe until Betty returned home. The garage door went up to let in her car around two in the afternoon. Betty was working half days in a medical clinic. She was a physician who had been a university professor, as I had, before we moved to Fort Atkinson. Betty had rushed home because she was planning to do a little shopping, which was definitely more interesting to her than work.

We were headed to Cambridge to visit the

pottery store. Cambridge was about ten miles down the road from Fort Atkinson. Before we started out, however, I had to buy Betty a Happy Meal at McDonald's. She never seemed to have time for lunch when she was working, so she was starving. We needed to get something for her quickly, so McDonald's was the best bet. Besides, sometimes she just got hungry for a Happy Meal. Actually, she really developed a periodic hankering for one of the toys that comes in a Happy Meal. When that happened, it was best not to be slow about providing one.

We drove up to the drive-through because Betty was convinced that she was committing a felony by ordering a child's meal when she was an adult. At the drive-through window, she could feign innocence. The conversation at the speaker box went something like this.

"May I help you, sir?"

"We would like one Happy Meal with a coke and one burger with a diet coke."

"What kind of hamburger, sir?"

"What kind is on the dollar menu?"

"Excuse me, sir?"

"The dollar menu! What kind of burger is

on the dollar menu?"

"A regular hamburger, sir."

"Then that's what I want."

"Excuse me, sir?"

"I. Want. A. Regular. Hamburger."

"What did you want to drink with that, sir?"

"A. Diet. Coke."

"Yes, sir. That will be five forty-nine."

"Wait!"

"Yes, sir?"

"We want a girl toy!"

"Excuse me, sir?"

"WE WANT A GIRL TOY IN THE HAPPY MEAL!" In the rear view mirror, I could see the people in the car behind me were laughing.

"Yes, sir. Please pull up to the next window."

When I pulled up to the next window, the cashier handed me the food and accepted my money. Betty was trying to make herself invisible by looking out the passenger window and pretending she was not in the car. When the Happy Meal was handed over I said, "It's not for me. I would have asked for a boy toy."

DEAD MAN IN HEAD

"Really, sir?" asked the cashier with a smile.

"That didn't sound quite right, but you know what I mean."

"Yes, sir. I think I do. Have a nice day."

When we drove away, there were several moments of silence. Finally, I announced, "I hate drive through-windows."

Betty did not answer at first. Then she said, "I am so humiliated."

"It's better to get out of the car and go in for your food. That way, they can at least understand what you want."

"Most people in the world can manage to use a drive-through window. You are the only one who has problems."

"Really?" Was it possible that she was correct on that point?

We rode in silence to the pottery store in Cambridge. Betty was determined to enjoy herself despite the fiasco at McDonald's, so she went in. I opted to stay outside and smoke my pipe.

Before lighting up, I cleaned the trash out of the car, stuffing it into a can by the door of the pottery store. Then I loaded my pipe, lit up, and leaned against the car to puff. After ten minutes or so, some other customers arrived. A young couple tossed their half-empty soda cups in the trash can. A family came by and threw in their fast food trash. This prompted a certain level of uneasiness in my mind, but I could not quite put my finger on what was bothering me.

I puffed a few more minutes when suddenly I realized my mistake: I had thrown away the McDonald's bag. Quickly, I searched the car for the girl toy. It was nowhere to be seen. This was an emergency. If, after all that embarrassment, Betty did not have her girl toy to show for the trip to McDonald's, my life would not be worth a plugged nickel.

There was no alternative. I went over to the trash can and plunged my arm in up to the shoulder, feeling around for the bag I had thrown in and the treasure within it. The side of my face was pushed against the cold metal of the trash can as I rooted around in its bowels like a gastroenterologist with a scope.

While I was so engaged, I heard a car drive up. Footsteps approached me. A voice spoke out somewhere beyond my left ear.

DEAD MAN IN HEAD

"So, Mr. Schumacher, you taking up dumpster diving?"

"First of all, this is not a dumpster. Dumpsters are bigger. Second, I'm not diving into it. I'm just feeling around. So this is not dumpster diving because it involves neither a dumpster nor diving. Any dodo should be able to tell that." Ordinarily, I was not that grumpy, but under the circumstances, anyone would have been testy.

Turning my head, I could finally identify the speaker. It was my old arch-enemy Sergeant Schmidt of the Fort Atkinson police department. She appeared to be very angry about the lack of respect I had shown her exalted position. Standing next to her was Sergeant Broder. He was trying to suppress a grin. Whether he was laughing at me for my awkward position, at Schmidt for having been on the losing end of a zinger, or me for the trouble I had caused myself by zinging Schmidt, was hard to determine. Most likely, it was all three.

Schmidt ground her teeth. "Listen, Schumacher. We don't have time for your guff. We're taking you back to Fort. We need to talk."

"Now?"

"Yes, right now. Get out of the trash can and get in your car. You can follow us back."

"Can't right now."

"Can't? What do you mean, can't? When we say 'go,' you 'go'." She was yelling now.

I couldn't go off and leave Betty in the store. And I couldn't give up on finding the girl toy. So I told a little white lie.

"Stuck."

Broder started to laugh.

"You want me to bring the trash can with me?" I asked. "I can't drive this way, but I can drag it into the back seat of your car."

Broder was guffawing while Schmidt sputtered with rage.

Fortunately, my hand closed on the girl toy at that moment and I was helped to pull my arm out of the can. "Ah, that was a close one," I said. Then Betty came out of the pottery store.

Broder explained the situation to her. "Mrs. Schumacher, we need to talk over a few matters with your husband. You can drive yourself home, can't you?"

DEAD MAN IN HEAD

Betty was fine with it. "No, I don't mind driving myself home. And, Sergeant," she said as he started to turn away. "Keep him as long as you like."

I had stuck my arm into a trash can for that woman and that was all the thanks I got. The world can be very unjust at times.

When we arrived at the city building in Fort Atkinson, Broder and Schmidt led me into the interview room. We sat down on opposite sides of a small wooden table. A television was in one corner of the room.

Broder began with some small talk. "You and the missus go over to Cambridge often?"

"Now and then. That's a nice spot down there, you know."

"Yes, it is. Oh, in case you were wondering, we knew you were there because there's an all-points out on your car and one of the locals called it in. Since the plates turned up your name, we said we would come get you. After all, we have gotten to know you pretty well over the last couple of years." He was referring to some contretemps that had arisen due to circumstances entirely beyond my control.

98

SHERLOCK HOLMES

'Why is there an APB out on my car?" I knew I had run a stop sign, but that did not seem like reason enough for an APB.

Schmidt suddenly slammed her fist onto the little table, making it shake and rattle. "Don't pretend to be innocent with us, you creep! Give us one good reason we shouldn't charge you right now with public endangerment?"

"Public endangerment? For running a stop sign?"

"No, you moron. For arson. You not only contributed to arson, you also cost the city of Madison a lot of money. They had to send two fire trucks and two patrol cars to the scene. The fire damage will run into the thousands. You are in big trouble and you better come clean with us."

"I have no idea what you're talking about."

She snorted. "I figured you would say that." She turned on the TV and fiddled with it a bit. "This was recorded this morning," she said. As we watched the screen brighten up, we could see a silver hatchback drive up next to a dumpster in an alley. Two seedy looking characters got out. One was talking on a cell

99

phone, while the other went out of sight. When he returned, he lit a cigarette, then set about starting a fire in the dumpster. He pulled the most flammable bits up where they could get some air and lit the pile in several places. The two seedy characters, one a pyromaniac and the other an idiot, got back in the car and drove away.

We sat in silence for a moment. Frankly, I was at a loss for words. The other two were just watching me think about the mess I was in. Finally, I rallied a bit.

"Okay, that was me alright. On the phone. But I didn't see the other guy lighting the fire. This is a complete surprise to me."

Schmidt sneered at me. "You expect us to believe that? A guy lights a bonfire right next to you and you don't even notice?"

At this point, Broder intervened. "Now, now, let's not get ahead of ourselves here. I think it is safe to say that Professor Schumacher here may be the only person in the state of Wisconsin who can provide a long series of documented instances where he did not notice what was going on around him. Anybody else who claimed not to notice the fire would get laughed at. Not the professor here."

"Thanks," I said to him. He was not offering me a compliment, but I would settle for mercy.

Broder turned to me. "We can let you get on with your day if you just tell us who that man was who set the fire and where he is now."

"Well, I can do one of those things. His name is Sherlock Holmes and he lives in the shelter in downtown Madison. But he ran off so I have no idea where he is now."

"Ran off?"

"Yes. We were eating lunch at Wendy's and he ran off." Broder looked doubtful. "Holmes has a history of mental illness," I added. That seemed to cause Broder to accept the story.

"All right then," he said. "I guess you can go now. Do you need a ride home or can you walk from here?"

"I can walk. No problem." If there had been three feet of snow outside, the answer would have been the same. I just wanted to get away from those guys.

DEAD MAN IN HEAD

Broder opened the door so I could leave. As I was walking out, his face grew puzzled and he asked, "what did you say to Holmes that made him run off?"

"It wasn't so much what I said as what he said. He practically admitted killing the fellow we found in the freezer last month."

The door slammed shut. Broder took me by the arm and led me back to my chair. The interview wasn't over after all. In fact, I didn't get to go home for a long time.

Betty was reading a book when I staggered into our living room after the long interrogation the police had imposed upon me. She did not look up when I entered the room. "Still mad at me?" I asked.

Betty gave me a cold stare. "Do I have a reason to be mad at you?"

"I embarrassed you at McDonald's. I'm sorry. I have trouble with drive-through windows."

She sighed, relenting a bit. "I know you do."

"Am I forgiven?"

"I'll think about it." She changed the subject. "What was that about with the police?

Are you in trouble again?"

Again? That seemed hardly fair. "The guy I interviewed in Madison today set fire to a dumpster. The police wanted to know his name and whereabouts."

"That seems pretty simple. Why did it take so long?"

"Well, at first they thought maybe I knew he was setting the fire."

Betty decided not to probe into the reasons behind that misunderstanding. "What else? You were there a very long time."

"Well, you remember the body in the freezer? The fellow I had lunch with today said something that sounded like he might have killed that guy."

"What?" she shouted. "You had lunch with a murderer? You might have been killed!"

"I was in no danger. We were at Wendy's, for Pete's sake."

"You know this kind of thing makes me crazy! You can't take risks like that! It's not fair to me!"

"I know. But don't you see: there was no way I could have known he was a murderer before we started having lunch."

DEAD MAN IN HEAD

Betty gave me a glare. "You're always scaring me."

"I'm sorry. I didn't mean to." We hugged and I think she forgave me. I hope so, anyway.

"Hey," I said. "This has been a rough day for both of us. How about if I make us a martini?"

"I'm way ahead of you, mister. I had a martini an hour ago."

Betty laughed at the disappointed expression on my face. "You can go ahead and make one for yourself, though."

While I mixed it up, she chatted with me. "You better believe I enjoyed that martini. It was just what I needed. Those pickled mushrooms were a little old though." Betty liked to put pickled mushrooms in her martini instead of olives. I never understood the attraction, but different strokes for different folks.

"I thought the pickled mushrooms were all gone."

"So did I, but you forgot to throw the jar away. I found it in the fridge with a couple of little bits of mushroom floating in the brine. With a couple of teaspoons of brine to make it a 'dirty' martini and those bits of mushroom, I think I may have invented a new drink. What should we call it?"

There was a long moment of silence while I considered my options. Finally, I said, "how about a Bucky Banger?"

"Oh, that sounds good." Betty liked the idea. I felt kind of sick, myself.

CHAPTER 8. THE VOICE IN THE NIGHT

The next morning I went through my usual routine. Start the coffee, shower, dress, pick up a newspaper at the convenience store, bring Betty her coffee and part of the paper. After Betty and I had finished the papers and she went off to work, I poured the last of the coffee into my cup and sat down in my living room chair. >From my Morris chair, I could see through the sliding glass door across the deck. The sky was a light blue with a few clouds. It looked to be a fine December day. Most likely, our downstairs neighbor, Emily Eberhardt, would take her dog out for a walk within the next hour. Emily was a reliable character who could be counted on for a sensible perspective on this complicated case. Immediately, I resolved to hold a council of war before finalizing my report. Emily, Andrew, and Betty could help me make some sense out of the available information.

Help was desperately needed because I was confused. While it seemed likely that Holmes had killed Miles Archer, a few loose ends remained. Like, why did he do it? Why was the body in a freezer and why was Holmes pushing the freezer across Main Street? And did this death have anything to do with the research project? Another fact occurred to me: Archer and Holmes were reputed to be bosom buddies. Why, then, would Holmes kill Archer?

Emily, Betty, and Andrew would be invaluable in helping me clarify the issues. However, one personal issue of my own was definitely not coming up for discussion because it was a secret that I had kept to myself for several years.

Betty had gone out of town on a business trip. Before she left we argued about something trivial. The first day of being a bachelor was quite pleasant. The second day was boring. The third day I started to get very uncomfortable. Edgy and restless, I took walks, tried watching television, ran errands, but nothing helped. Finally, about nine p.m. I gave it up and went to bed, even though I was not sleepy. Shortly after I lay down, I heard a voice say my name.

Quite frankly, it spooked me. The voice had sounded like it was in my bedroom. It could have been either a man or a woman. It was clear and loud. Somehow it contained a note of mocking humor, as if there was something very amusing about the situation.

I got up and searched the house. I looked over the deck, thinking that perhaps someone was down below on the sidewalk, calling up to me. There was no one around anywhere.

A dream, you say? This was extremely real. No dream in my experience had ever had this quality of reality.

Of course, I had to consider the possibility that I was out of my mind. Hearing voices was the classic symptom, after all. One thing was very clear to me, unfortunately: that voice was so real that if I heard it very often I would not be able to convince myself that it was imaginary. It might all be in my head. Even so, it would be as real as anything else that I could perceive.

Getting back to sleep took a long time

since I was scared out of my wits. Eventually, I dropped off. The voice never came back. But I never forgot the experience. It was one of my most indelible memories.

The investigation I was currently pursuing made me think about that voice. How different was I, really, than Doc Watson and the others? How much of a push would it take to tip me over into their circumstances? And could it happen to the average person? Could it happen to you?

Honestly, I did not know how close I was to serious mental illness. Nor could I say how much stress was required before the average person would lose his tenuous grip on reality. Maybe we all had demons in the back of our minds that we actively sought to repress at a subconscious level. Given a weak moment, the demons might escape. Then we would be the ones locked in the hospital, trapped in a group home, or evicted from a homeless center.

Our natural tendency is to avoid thinking about people with serious mental illness. This is shortsighted. There but for the grace of God go you, me, or our loved ones. If and when it happens, we will wish we had done more to

create a safety net that allows even the most
confused person to live comfortably and safely
in a world that is filled with terrors.

CHAPTER 9. INTERVIEW WITH ARCHY MCNALLY

That day I went in search of the last research subject, Archy McNally. McNally was recorded as living in Milton, which was about twenty minutes south of Fort Atkinson on Highway 26. No one answered the door at his apartment. His work address was listed as the local Goodwill store, so that was where I went next.

McNally was working the checkout counter. He was a thin, nervous young man in his late twenties. When I said I needed a few minutes of his time, he called in a substitute to watch the register and we went outside, where he immediately lighted a cigarette.

"What can I do for you?" he asked.

I ran through my spiel about the research project.

"Yeah," he said. "I remember the project. I signed up for it on purpose."

DEAD MAN IN HEAD

"Why did you agree to be in the project?"

"Because they asked me to. I was being helpful."

"You had no concerns about the purpose of the project?"

"You mean about maybe being cured of seeing dead people? That was what I wanted to happen. I wanted to get my life back on track. By doing everything the doctors and nurses and social workers want, you get to move on with your life. And because I did that, I have this job and I have an apartment."

"That's great. It sounds like you are doing really well."

McNally waved his arms around excitedly. "I'm doing great!" he said, shifting his feet around excitedly. "And after this I'm going to law school, then I'll run for Congress. Who knows, maybe I'll be the first guy to run for president who was ever in psych treatment."

"Actually, there was one guy I remember. A vice presidential candidate. The news stories said he had been treated for serious problems with depression."

"Really? I never heard of that."

"Well, it was before your time. You're a

young guy. You have plenty of time to accomplish your goals."

This got McNally back on his theme. He started waving his arms again. "That's right. On track. First law school, then Congress, then the Oval Office."

"I wish you luck."

McNally stared at me hard for a moment. Perhaps he suspected that I did not rate his chances of being president too highly.

"Oh, by the way, Archy," I said. "Did you know Miles Archer was dead? Somebody put him in a freezer. Did you hear about that?"

McNally was withdrawing, looking over his shoulder to see if anyone could overhear our conversation. "No, I didn't hear that," he said.

"Do you have ideas on who might have done it?"

He actually jumped, as if he had been stabbed with a pin. "No. No idea."

"Do you think Sherlock Holmes might have done it?"

McNally's reaction surprised me. Instead of getting more anxious, he actually relaxed when he heard the question.

"Did Holmes kill Archer? No way, man."

"Why are you so sure?"

"Well, they were good buddies. Holmes would have done anything for Archer. And besides, Holmes wouldn't hurt a fly. He looks scary, but that's just an act. He runs like a rabbit whenever he gets a little nervous. And everything makes him nervous."

I laughed. "Yeah, I know what you mean about him running like a rabbit. But if he didn't do it, who did?"

"That's obvious. It was the dead people, of course."

My jaw dropped open. McNally immediately recognized his error. "Ah, just kidding. There aren't any dead people. Just testing you! Ha, ha! Hey, I gotta go now. Catchya later, man." And he ran back into the Goodwill   store.

CHAPTER 10. INTERVIEW WITH DR. ZELICOV

My final interview was with Milo Zelicov, MD, who was the genius who dreamed up the research project I was investigating. Even before meeting with him, I assumed the man was an incompetent researcher. His project was ill-conceived and, based on the interviews completed up to now, most of the 'subjects' had not met the standards of 'informed consent': they either did not know they had signed up, did not know what they had signed up for, or denied that they had ever signed up.

Since I was a few minutes early, I stopped at a McDonald's for a coffee on my way into Madison from Fort Atkinson. In my mind, I imagined what response I would receive if I discussed Zelicov with the crowd of elderly folks who were holding down chairs and coffee cups in one corner of the restaurant. The conversation would have gone something like this.

DEAD MAN IN HEAD

Geezer 1: "Are you tellin' me....."

Ed: "Yessireebob."

Geezer 2: "Oh m'gosh, you can't mean it."

Ed: "It's the God's honest truth."

Geezer 3: "Well geewhilikers. Don't that just beat all."

Ed: "Don't it, now?"

Geezer 1: "It's a free country. You can do what you want. But if people'd grow a brain they would plan ahead better, if you know what I mean. That's my opinion. It's just my opinion but that's what I think. No point in beatin' 'bout the bush on these matters."

Geezers 2 and 3: "You can say that again. Yup."

Feeling reinforced by my imaginary conversation with the geezers, who were sure to agree with me if we actually had discussed it, I was ready for my meeting with Zelicov. I was 'loaded for bear,' as the geezers would have put it.

Zelicov's office was in the Department of Psychiatry and Psychology of the Medical University of Madison. This told me he probably was expected to see patients in addition to doing his research. If he had been in a liberal arts college, I would have classified him as a teacher, rather than a clinician.

A secretary directed me toward Zelicov's office, which turned out to be an examination room. A vinyl-clad chair was placed in front of a small metal desk on which a computer terminal sat. Another chair was placed next to the desk. You could almost visualize a patient and his wife, or a patient and her husband, or a patient and her mother sitting in those chairs, anxious and perhaps defensive. This, clearly, was a room in which patients were seen and the information taken from them was entered directly into the computer. If any research went on in that room, it clearly was not regarded as the most important activity. An office where research was a priority would have had a bigger desk and it would not have needed two chairs for visitors, especially not chairs upholstered in vinyl. Vinyl was used when the occupants of the chairs were likely to be wet or dirty or destructive.

The chair that was placed behind the desk and in front of the computer was occupied by a small man with a goatee who was wearing a long white coat. He welcomed me with a gesture toward one of the chairs and a warm smile.

"Professor Schumacher! How good of you to come," he said cheerfully. For a moment I forgot that I was the one who had requested the meeting.

"Doctor Zelicov," I said as I offered my hand to him. "Thank you for being available on such short notice."

"Delighted, delighted, I'm sure. This is a very serious matter. One which will be easy to clear up, but when the federal government is demanding answers, one doesn't dilly-dally, no?"

"Not if one is smart," was my reply.

Zelicov slapped his knee and laughed. "Yes, yes. Quite right you are. But first, the amenities. Amenities are very important to good working relationships, I find. So, would you like some coffee? There is one coffee pot in the area that has excellent coffee. It is the personal machine of a colleague of mine. He will let us share some, if you like. Come, I will send for it, yes?"

"That would be nice."

Zelicov made a brief call, then put the

phone down and leaned back in his chair. "You live near here, I understand, in the town of Fort Atkinson?"

"That's correct. We moved there recently from the panhandle of Texas."

"Yes, I detected an accent there. But you are not originally from Texas, I think. Somewhere in the Midwest, perhaps?"

"Very good. Yes, I am from Indiana originally."

"And you are some kind of government investigator?"

We were interrupted by the arrival of our coffee. It came in porcelain mugs, not Styrofoam cups. The aroma was rich, but the coffee turned out to be flavored. I tried not to grimace when swallowing it.

"Government investigator? Not really. I describe myself as a consulting research ethicist, which is a niche I fell into by accident. This is my first case in which the federal government asked for my services."

"A consulting research ethicist?" Zelicov was nonplussed. "Forgive me, but that sounds a bit pretentious."

"It sounds pretentious if you focus on the

119

ethicist part because the title suggests that the consultant pretends to be more ethical than anyone else. In practice, however, many people are experts in research ethics. Every conscientious researcher thinks about ethics. Every member of a research review board, and there are many, thinks about ethics. All of us who have served on those boards have been trained to look for certain rules to be followed. Was the patient shown respect? Was he lied to? Was he fully informed about the project before he agreed to participate? Did the risks exceed the benefits? Was confidentiality protected? These rules are so clear that any researcher can learn them. That is not the hard part about being a consulting research ethicist."

Zelicov pondered for a moment. "You make an interesting case. But do go on: what is the important skill required by a research ethicist?"

"You have to be an experienced researcher. Experience matters because it helps you judge the most important issue: do the likely benefits of the research exceed the risks to the human guinea pigs? And I don't mean the benefits expected by the researcher because that person has trouble being objective about the benefits of his own project. Besides, he might be an inexperienced researcher and not realize that his research plan is flawed. If the research design is flawed, then no benefits are likely to result, which means even a low risk project should not be undertaken."

"I see. You are here to judge the quality f my research." Zelicov had gone pale.

"I don't pretend to be an expert in your field of research. On the other hand, the general principles of good research design are well-accepted. I would not be able to tell if your theory is wrong."

He relaxed a little at that. "Now I understand. This begins to make some sense to me." He spread his hands wide. "So, ask your questions."

"First, let me address the issue of informed consent."

"Yes, yes, of course. All of the subjects were explained about the project. They all signed the forms in front of a witness."

"These were psych patients. Some were

heavily medicated. Did you take any special steps to ensure that they understood what they were signing?"

"We explained the project to them until we were sure they understood. We are experienced clinicians; we can judge when a person understands what he is being told."

"Let's take a few of the subjects and deal with them specifically. Do you remember them?"

"I reviewed the files in preparation for this meeting."

"Okay, Lew Archer."

"Yes, Mr. Archer. He happens to be an inpatient again right now. I know him well."

"You consented him yourself?"

"Yes, I did. He understood perfectly."

"Were you present when he signed the form?"

"Yes, of course."

I said nothing at that point. Instead, I just sat there and looked at him. Zelicov looked back calmly at first, then the cogs in his brain began turning over. The moment when he remembered what actually happened when Lew Archer was consented was obvious: he turned pale again. Then he had to decide whether to lie to me or confess. He chose to do neither.

"Dr. Zelicov, did you actually see Lew Archer sign the form?"

"Well, that was a long time ago. I don't actually remember. Why do you question it?"

"Because he does not remember, he is generally uncooperative, and the handwriting looks exactly like his mother's and not like his own."

Zelicov was sweating. "I see your point," he said.

"It turns out that the other patients don't remember consenting, deny that they would have consented, or say that their consent was predicated on anticipated rewards. You know, I'm sure, that offering rewards for consenting can be coercive. I'm forced to conclude that your consenting process did not follow approved procedures."

"I'm sorry you have reached that conclusion. However, I am sure you realize that this is a tempest in a teapot, so to speak. The project was risk-free. No one was hurt."

"Someone died."

"That could not have been caused by the research!"

"Couldn't it? These were mentally impaired patients, highly vulnerable. You were undermining delusions that might have been important to them." I held up my hand to stop his protests. "No, stop there. I understand that the therapeutic process is intended to address those delusions. But this was a research project. It must be held to a higher standard. To say that there was no risk at all is simply not true. What we have to address is this: was the risk greater than the likely benefits?"

Zelicov was still trying to put up a brave front, but it was obvious he could tell he was doomed. "The potential benefits were enormous," he whispered.

"You mean curing delusions? The chances of that resulting from this project appear to be nil."

"Nil?" He was aghast.

"You had no control group. Your sample size was too small to lead to any conclusions."

"This was a pilot study! Those issues don't apply to a pilot study!"

"Even a pilot project should offer more

benefits than risks. If you weren't going to learn anything from doing the project, then you shouldn't have done the project. The university should not have permitted you to do the project."

He held his head in his hands.

"Dr. Zelicov," I said. "How much research experience do you have?"

"I worked as a laboratory assistant back in Moscow before coming to the United States. Here, I have been a busy clinician. Too busy with patients to do research."

"Why did you change direction and try to do this project?"

"The university has been pressuring everyone to get research grants. And if we get grants, our patient load will be reduced."

"You're a little burned out on seeing psych patients?"

"You have no idea," he said.

I had to sympathize with the guy. But I also had to bar him from research if I could manage it. As a researcher, the man was a menace. I hoped he was better as a clinician, but somehow it seemed unlikely.

CHAPTER 11. THE REPORT

Andrew, Emily Eberhardt, Betty, and I convened our meeting in the evening after my meeting with Zelicov. None of them had heard all of the details of the case and Emily had heard none of the story before that night. First drinks were handed out to everybody, beer for the men and wine for the women. Then I started talking. After I had summed it all up for them, Andrew voiced an opinion.

"Ed," he said. "It sounds like you have already made up your mind about what you are going to say in your report. You are going to come down hard on Zelicov. So, what do you want from us?"

Betty chimed in at that point. "Do you just want us to say you are right? There must be more to this meeting than that." Emily was looking a bit disgruntled as well. To avoid a rebellion, I rushed ahead.

"Hey, you guys, calm down. I really do

need your help. For one thing, I might be biased and if I am you will be able to talk me out of my position. For another thing, there might be some issues involved that I have not considered. And the most interesting problem is one that I have no solution to: who killed Miles Archer and why? As long as we don't know the answer to that question I will have to wonder if we aren't missing something important to the investigation. A research subject is dead and we don't know why. How can we be sure that the research project did not lead to his death? If so, then my report would be seriously flawed for failing to say so." With that, I leaned back in my chair and waited for a reaction. I didn't have to wait very long.

Betty spoke up immediately. "Basically, you feel like you can safely say that the research project should not have been approved by the university in the first place, and also that Zelicov broke all the rules when he recruited his patients into it. So, let's just agree that your report will be very critical on those points. But the more important issue has to do with the relationships between families and patients and how they might have been affected."

Emily agreed. "That's right," she said. "Those relationships must have been strained or even destroyed by the stresses affecting them. If the project hurt the relationships, that is the most important issue. But if it helped, then we can forgive the professor for breaking a few rules."

Betty added more at that point. "The fears the parents had for their family members might have been reduced if the project offered some hope. Who cares if the hope was a pipedream? All that matters is that something was being attempted that might offer a slim chance of a cure. Eventually those families have to move on with their lives. They have to forgive themselves and everyone else so that they can rebuild what's left of their lives."

Andrew was looking at his shoes. "Do you understand what the heck they are talking about?" I asked him.

"Sort of," he answered

"No kidding? Then maybe you can explain it to me."

"It sounds sort of like something I heard on Oprah."

"You watch Oprah?"

THE REPORT

"No, but once when I was channel hopping her show came up. They were talking bout that stuff."

"Which stuff?"

"You know. Relationships."

Betty was outraged. "Men! You don't understand anything. How do they get through life?" she asked Emily.

"Women have to do it for them," was the answer she got back.

"Hey, if you wise women want to write down something for me that I can put in the report on this relationship stuff, I will be glad to put it in. Right now I'm clueless, though."

"You got that right, Buddy," Betty said.

I couldn't let her have the last word. "Look, from my point of view, what matters is whether the patients get to live their lives the way they want. Forget about some dream of a cure. If they want to have jobs, then they should be able to work. If they want to control their delusions, they should have meds. If they want a place of their own to live in, they should have it."

"Where can people work if they have a serious mental illness?" Andrew asked.

Betty had an answer for that. "Wal-Mart hires them sometimes."

This brought up the debate that seemed to be going on forever in Fort Atkinson about whether to let Wal-Mart open a store in the county. The critics were still winning the fight, but some of their arguments were starting to sound a little off-base.

Emily chimed in at this point. "We don't want a lot of low-wage jobs coming in here. Besides it will put the local businesses out of business."

"You don't see them hiring the mentally ill," I replied. "The local businesses claim that Wal-Mart is bad because it doesn't offer health insurance, but neither do they. In fact, it doesn't matter about the health insurance. All the big corporations will start backing away from their health insurance plans eventually. Wal-Mart just got there first."

"I suppose you think we should have a national health insurance program anyway," Andrew said.

"Sure, that's what I think, but I know we won't get one." It would be cheaper for everybody and everybody would have coverage, but it's just not the American way."

"Then what is going to happen when all the corporations stop offering health insurance benefits?" Andrew asked.

"Then most medical care becomes a cash business," I answered. "We will buy services on ebay for very low prices. When we get sick, we will send an email message to our health care company, they will try to deal with us by sending us prescriptions without ever actually seeing us or even talking to us. If we insist on talking to someone, it will mean a long distance call to India or somewhere like that."

Betty was not too concerned. "So what? Doctors like me can't cure most of the problems people see us for. Genetics and unhealthy habits shorten our lives and medical care can't make much of a difference."

That remark, coming from a doctor, left the rest of us speechless for a moment.

"Well," I said, "at least we can agree that psychotic people are helped by getting their meds." That point brought no arguments from anyone. But nobody had much confidence that the government would always be willing to pay for those meds.

DEAD MAN IN HEAD

Emily had the last word to say before we broke up the group. "Ed," she said. "You say that the research project was so weak it had no hope of doing any good. That means it could not have done much harm either. So maybe the whole thing is a tempest in a teapot."

After Andrew and Emily left, I set to work writing up the report. Basically, it just said that the project should not have been approved and the rights of the research subjects were not protected. It also said that while the cause of death for one of the subjects was unknown, it probably was not caused by the research. I recommended that Zelicov be barred from research and that the university undergo an exhaustive audit by the feds to see if they were failing to protect the rights of research subjects involved in other projects. I sent the report to the university as an email attachment then washed my hands of it. Overall, the final report for this case was extremely unsatisfying.

CHAPTER 12. CHRISTMAS PARTY AT DOC'S

When Betty and I pulled into Doc Watson's driveway on Christmas Eve, there was another car already there. I wondered who it could be. As far as I knew, none of the other people who were expected to attend our little party owned cars. When I called Doc and offered to buy take-out chicken for an informal get-together, he said he would round up Sherlock, Lew Archer, Archie Goodwin and Archy McNally. Miss Marple was assumed to be too ill to attend. This was a two-bucket party. I chose one bucket of crispy and one of regular.

Everyone else was present when Doc let us in. Doc introduced everyone to Betty. One person was present whom I had not met. He was introduced as Mycroft Holmes, Sherlock's brother. Mycroft had a short haircut and was wearing a sport coat and slacks, with an open

DEAD MAN IN HEAD

collared dress shirt. He appeared to be a quiet man, somber but with obvious intelligence. He was a bit on the portly side and bore no resemblance to his brother Sherlock at all.

Distributing paper plates, napkins, and chicken did not take long. Soon everyone was munching happily. A cooler of beer was under the table, so within twenty minutes, the sound of smacking lips was supplemented with occasional belches.

Eventually, Betty and I could eat no more. Mycroft had stopped after one piece. I gathered that take-out chicken was not part of his usual diet.

When he saw that we were finished, Mycroft stood up and cleared his throat. "Gentlemen," he said, "and Mrs. Schumacher" he added with a nod to Betty. "We have a little business to take care of." He pulled a fold of papers out of his jacket pocket. "As you know, I am the executor of Miles Archer's will. Now that the police have closed the investigation of Mr. Archer's death, we can settle the estate."

I raised my hand. "Hold on a minute, Mycroft. First, I didn't know the police investigation was over. Second, if you are going to read a will, then Betty and I should leave because we didn't even know Miles Archer." I started to stand, but Mycroft held up his hand to stop me.

"Professor Schumacher," he said, "please wait. All will be made clear to you. And I assure you that your presence here is appropriate."

As I settled back down in my chair, I sensed that, aside from Betty, everyone else in the room was aware of what Mycroft was going to say.

"First, of all, I should provide a little background. My brother Sherlock and Miles Archer were friends, so two years ago when Sherlock brought Mr. Archer to me for the purpose of making up a will, I agreed to do so, even though the case was assumed to be pro bono and there might be some who would question whether Mr. Archer was of sound mind. However, since Mr. Archer had no heirs, I thought it would be safe and appropriate to accede to his wishes, despite their somewhat unusual nature." Mycroft consulted his papers with a frown, then proceeded with his oration.

"Mr. Archer wanted his assets to be placed

in trust in the event of his death. The purpose of the trust was very clear: Mr. Archer wanted the trust to provide support to persons who were in a special minority group. Mr. Archer called that minority group "persons with radically alternative perceptions of reality who have financial difficulties due to those perceptions." He wanted the trust to provide housing and cash assistance to eligible persons in such a manner when two requirements were met. First, the assets would not be transferred to payees in amounts that were sufficiently large so as to jeopardize disability payments. Second, the assistance provided to payees would in no way restrict their freedom. Mr. Archer understood that sometimes difficult judgments would be required to carry out the intent of the will, so he specified that a director of the trust be chosen who was acceptable to a board of persons he regarded as trustworthy. To wit, these gentlemen." Mycroft looked up, then waved his hand in the direction of Lew Archer, Doc Watson, Sherlock, Archie Goodwin and Archy McNally, all of whom applauded.

Turning to me, Mycroft asked, "Professor

Schumacher, do you have any questions so far?"

"I'm too fascinated to have questions. Maybe later."

"Then we will continue. Each member of the board of the trust has interviewed a candidate for the director position. All have found this candidate to be acceptable to them. If the candidate accepts the position, then we have some forms to sign. Professor Schumacher, the board would like to offer the position to you. Do you have any questions now?"

Betty gasped. "Wait a minute," I said. "When did these interviews take place?"

"You spoke to each of the board members."

"But I was interviewing them!"

"If you like. They choose to view it as the other way around."

"But the police were still investigating Archer's death, so the will had not been read yet when I spoke to them."

"True, but not relevant to the board. They know now that they needed to conduct interviews so they choose to consider the meetings with you as meeting the requirement." Mycroft hesitated, then added with a twinkle in his eye, "the members of the board are not as committed to conventional views of space and time as are most governing boards." That was certainly an understatement. He went on. "Do you think you might be willing to accept the position?"

I turned to look at the board members. "Doc, do you think this is a good idea?"

Doc smiled. "You're one of us, man."

"Lew?"

"You a fool, but you not stupid."

"You mean, I'm ignorant but teachable?"

Lew smiled at me as I used to smile at a grad student who provided the correct answer in class. "That's what I mean."

"Archie Goodwin?"

"You get my vote. And I'm first in line for some help. Get me out that group home. It's nasty."

"Archy McNally?"

"Sure. But I don't need any help for myself."

"Of course. Sherlock?"

"The legs are all gone," he replied. Sherlock

was feeling around in the chicken bucket.

Next I turned back to Mycroft. "I'm touched and honored at the trust these folks have in me. But I must ask a question. Is there any money in this trust? Would I be taking on a responsibility without the means of accomplishing anything?"

He obviously had been waiting for me to ask this question. "Mr. Archer had been a successful stockbroker for several years before he was first hospitalized. After that, he became homeless, but most of his assets remained intact, at least at first. At the time he came to me to make out his will, he had just converted all of his funds into a cash purchase of a single stock. This was a new stock offering. Mr. Archer spent all of his money on that stock in the belief that it would increase in value and thus provide the resources for the trust he envisioned."

Mycroft stopped at this point. All the eyes in the room were on me. I took a breath, then hazarded a guess. "Was it Google?"

Everyone in the room applauded me except Betty, who asked "what's so special about Google stock?"

DEAD MAN IN HEAD

"It went up. A lot." Turning to Mycroft, I said, "that answers the question. The trust has enough funds to do some good."

"Please understand that the director is limited to a salary of ten thousand dollars per year."

"That seems fair." I looked at Betty and she nodded. "I accept the position."

After that, Doc handed out presents to us all. He even had one for Betty. She got a chipped flower vase, about two inches tall. She said it was beautiful. Sherlock got a carton of cigarettes. The two Archies and Lew each got a small brown paper sack, which they accepted with enthusiasm. Mycroft got a tie clip. And Doc handed me a cap made out of aluminum foil. "Keeps out the radio waves," he said, deadpan. Everybody laughed.

After we had admired our gifts, I remembered the big, unanswered question. "Hey, wait a minute you guys. Nobody explained to me what happened to Miles Archer."

Mycroft looked at Sherlock and waited, but Sherlock was ignoring him. Mycroft sighed, then said, "The police picked up Sherlock shortly after the dumpster fire. I was called to represent him, as usual. Eventually, we were able to put together the facts that enabled the authorities to close the file on Miles Archer." Mycroft took a breath, then began the story that I had been waiting to hear since I was pulled out of the river.

"Mr. Archer felt that his alternative perception of reality was becoming too much of a burden for him. He believed that the only hope of escaping the visitations he experienced was to place himself behind some heavy shielding, such as by getting into a freezer. He found a freezer on a vacant lot that seemed to belong to no one, so he took advantage of the opportunity. The temperature was below zero that night."

"Didn't he understand that climbing into the freezer would be fatal?"

Mycroft looked at me with pity. "Of course he understood. He asked Sherlock to push the freezer into the river to provide additional shielding. Sherlock was irritated with him and tried to talk him out of it. They parted ways. When Sherlock returned to the freezer in the morning, he found Miles inside, dead.

DEAD MAN IN HEAD

Sherlock decided to carry out his friend's last wishes. And that is how he met you. You were helping carry out Miles Archer's last wishes. This is where the board's flexible attitude toward time comes into play again. You see, from the point of view of the board members, you accepted the position of trust director at that time. What happened today was merely an administrative detail from their point of view."

And maybe they were right. Shortly after that, the board members opened their brown paper sacks and took out baggies packed with something that they started rolling into cigarettes. Betty, Mycroft, and I decided it was time for us to leave. Mycroft announced that he would come around the next morning to pick up anyone who needed a ride home. He was told to make it after noon.

CHAPTER 13. CONCLUSION

The next few weeks were a lot of fun since I was spending someone else's money. Archy McNally and Archie Goodwin each got a trailer to live in, at the expense of the trust, and startup funds for their own ebay businesses. We also bought a trailer for Sherlock to live in, but his was consumed in a fire within a week. After that, I learned that the reason he had been evicted from the first homeless shelter was an unfortunate disagreement about a trash can fire. My next step was to buy a surplus storage canister from the Army. It was left over from Desert Storm. It was about the size of a mobile home and had been outfitted with a toilet and a metal door. The whole thing was metal. There was no way Sherlock could burn it down.

I also bought an old taxi for Lew Archer. His job was to be a driver for the other guys. He really enjoyed the role. He was never in a hurry to get anywhere and so was a safe driver. How often he actually took people where they wanted to go was unclear to me, but nobody complained. Maybe they all just enjoyed driving around.

We were starting to find new customers for the trust to help. Our board members recruited them in mysterious ways. Usually, Mycroft would just call and say that Doc had found another one. We would meet at McDonald's and discuss the person's needs and limitations, then Mycroft would write out a check for whatever goods or services we thought might be useful and appreciated.

The university received a public wrist-slap from the feds, but that news story was quickly forgotten. Presumably they went back to their old ways.

Betty complained that she was never able to reproduce the taste of the original Bucky Banger Martini, so she retired the name. She was happy that I was enjoying my new job as a director of a charitable trust.

"You seem to get along awfully well with those guys," she noticed.

"They are a lot of fun."

CONCLUSION

"Birds of a feather."

"That's why you like me."

"What do you mean?"

"If I was entirely normal, I wouldn't be as interesting."

"Interesting is an understatement," she said. But she was smiling when she said it.

Bucky proceeded to get fatter and fatter. Fritter got thinner and thinner. Betty said that Bucky was not letting her eat her share of the food. I put her dish up on the kitchen counter, but she preferred to eat down on the floor with him, even when he bullied her out of the way. He wasn't being deliberately cruel to her, just insensitive. He pursued his appetite in a clueless way, not noticing how much harm he was causing his house mate. Betty said that was just like the behavior of males of any species.

Of course, that made me wonder if I was causing her harm in an unthinking way. If being unthinking was the problem, then I would cure it by thinking. So, I thought about it and could not see any way to improve right away, so I quit worrying about it. But I resolved to try harder to be alert to the possible adverse consequences of my actions.

DEAD MAN IN HEAD

Betty was a Nervous Nelly, so anytime I went on an adventurous investigation it made her anxious. Next time, I would try harder not to worry her. But, heck, the only way to keep her from worrying would be to stay in the condo and not come out. A guy can't live that way all the time. At least, I couldn't.

We discussed all this. She decided, as usual, to forgive me for being, as she said, 'a galoot.' What more could a guy ask, after all, than a woman who would forgive him for being a galoot?